Whispers from the Swamp

∞

To Maddie,

There are more dangers in the swamp than just the alligators.

♡
Cavana

WHISPERS FROM THE SWAMP

C. A. Varian

Luna And Charlie Press

Talladega, Alabama

To my family,

Thank you so much for the support! I love y'all!

Contents

Cajun Pronunciations

Cormier: Cär mē ā
Cher: shă (pet name, means darling)
Boudreaux: Boo dro
Zydeco: zīdə ko
Jambalaya: jam bə lī ə
Bourgeois: boor ZHwä
Ledet: Lə dā
Richard: Rē shärd
Landry: Lan drē
Barrilleaux: Bär I lo
Babin: Bä bin
Chiasson: Shä sôn
Gautreaux: Go tro
Crawfish: krô fish
Breaux: Bro

Familiar Nightmares

Sounds of the road filled her ears as her eyes saw only blackness. The cloth against her tongue tasted of sweat and dust, but she could not push it away, forcing her to gag against it. The car jerked along the road as it hit ruts and potholes. She guessed it was not paved. Something about the moment felt familiar, like she had experienced it once before, but had somehow survived the ordeal. The air in the trunk thinned, causing her breath to come in short bursts and her head to spin. She tried to remain stoic, to fight her emotions as much as she planned to fight her captor, but her eyes betrayed her, allowing her backstabbing tears to reveal her fear.

As the car slowed to a stop, she wiped at her tears, attempting to harden her look before the trunk opened and revealed her as a weak, sobbing mess. She needed to fight.

Trying to shift her weight, to stretch her legs before fighting for her life, she kicked something large on the other side of the space. The mass budged only slightly against her feet, but she could not see what she was touching. Panic swelled in her chest as though a hand squeezed her heart.

The brakes squeaked as the car pulled to a stop, and the driver only took a second to climb out of the car and slam the driver's side door. She started to hyperventilate. The footsteps were nearly silent as they approached the trunk, making her think they were parked on a soft surface, like mud or dirt.

The setting sun barely lit the interior of the trunk as the door flung open, leaving her captor in shadow. She knew it was a man, but she could not make out his face.

Chancing a glance at her feet, she stifled a scream when she saw what she had been trying to kick. A woman, long chocolate hair and amber eyes staring sightlessly at the darkening sky, laid dead by her feet. Struggling to scoot her body away from the corpse, she expected the man to grab her, to kill her, but he only grabbed the dead woman and slammed the trunk door above her head, shutting her back into darkness.

***

Jolting awake, Hazel flung herself into a sitting position in the bed, feeling around herself to ensure her hands and feet were not bound. She closed her eyes, trying to make sense of her nightmare.

Another memory. The dead woman who was outside the building... it was her. But she was not one of Raymond Waters' victims... was she?

1

Honey Island Swamp Murders

Hazel Watson and Candy Townsend sat on the sofa, watching the local news. Hazel was still leaning towards leaving her career at the Public Defender's Office, but she scanned through her case files to prepare for an upcoming court date, anyway. Until she quit, she had to carry on with her career as expected. The news played, but she had practically zoned out to focus on her paperwork and was no longer paying attention to the broadcast until breaking news pulled her away from the documents on her lap. Raising the volume of the television, she leaned in closer.

"The bodies of two women were found in the Honey Island swamp area. One body has been identified as thirty-four-year-old New Orleans native Malerie Ledet. Authorities have not released the identity of the second victim. The police have no suspects at this time. If you have any tips, please contact the number on your screen," said the female news broadcaster.

Hazel's heart felt heavy, and a sour taste rose in her mouth. Swallowing hard, she began biting her nails. She knew that face. The woman's face on the television was the same face haunting her dreams, the same ghostly face she had seen reaching out for her outside of her apartment a few weeks before. She had ignored the spirit of Malerie Ledet then.

At the time, with Candy and Jake's killer on the loose, she could not imagine obligating herself to one more murder victim's spirit, even if she was born to help them. Malerie's spirit had reached out to her, practically begging for her help, but Hazel had looked at the ground and bolted into her apartment building. It was not like she did not feel guilty about it, but there was only so much she could handle. Especially when she was working a stressful full-time job as a public defender and battling post-traumatic stress within her own mind. Always letting spirits run her life had worn her down, and she couldn't do it anymore.

She did not need to see the face of the second victim. She already knew her name. Emily Landry. Although she had never seen Emily's spirit in person, Emily had invaded Hazel's subconscious mind on more than one occasion, traumatizing her through her dreams. Emily Landry had likely been abducted from her own backyard, a place where she planted a garden and played with her young daughter, Bella. Hazel did not have the closest relationship with her own parents as an adult, especially with them living across the country, but she could not imagine losing her mom at only seven years old. That was the unfortunate fate of Bella, Emily's daughter.

Hazel's heart hurt for the little girl.

I have to help them... both of them.

The crime reeked of Raymond Waters, the man who had abducted and nearly killed Hazel only a few months prior. Raymond had set his sights on her when she became tangled in the case of a missing woman who died at his hands. Hazel had taken too many risks when she looked into Angela Spencer's killer and, against her better judgement, had snuck into his house to look for evidence against him. Returning to his home while she was inside, he caught her there, hit her over the head, shoved her into the trunk of his car, and trapped her in his old fishing cabin until he returned to finish her off. She was forced to kill him in self-defense, an act she was still trying to come to terms with, but she had no choice. Raymond had killed four women and buried them in the swamp. He was a monster, and only one of them could survive. If it had not been for the spirits of his victims, she wouldn't have survived.

The crime being broadcasted had the hallmarks of Raymond, but it could not have been him. Shuddering at the thought, she lowered the volume on the television.

Did Raymond have a partner?

Just the thought of it made her want to vomit. Raymond could not have killed those two women. He had been dead for months. She bit her cheek as the heaviness pulled on her stomach, stopping only when she tasted blood. All murder investigations had one thing in common—murderers, and she would prefer to stay away from them.

"I've seen her," Hazel muttered to her spectral best friend, Candy.

"What's that?" Candy asked, pausing the television with a flourish of her hand before turning to face Hazel.

"I've seen her... well, both of them. They didn't name the other victim, but I'm positive her name is Emily."

Candy's blue eyes widened. She knew exactly what Hazel meant. Hazel had not seen the women alive. She had seen them after death.

"When did you see them? And where? Not in the apartment, I hope." Candy glanced around the room.

Although Candy was a spirit, she was not keen

on other spirits entering their apartment. The only other spirit she allowed in was Jake, but he was the recently murdered love of her life, so he did not count. Candy and Hazel had briefly checked into methods to keep other spirits out, but they had not come across any way to do that without also keeping out those spirits who were welcomed in their personal space, including Candy herself.

Hazel shook her head.

"No. I haven't technically seen either in our apartment, but I have had spirit-induced dreams of Emily. I don't know if that means she is in here and not manifesting, or if she is sending them from somewhere else. I've also seen Malerie in my dreams, as well as outside of the apartment building, but not inside."

Candy covered her face with her hands, cursing under her breath. "Damn. So, I guess that means they could possibly be visiting us without us seeing them. Ugh. I don't like it."

"I know. Neither do I."

Although she did not like unwelcome spirits in her house, Hazel had seen spirits since she was a child. It was a gift she inherited from the maternal line of her family, although it did not always feel like a gift to her. Although an introvert, she had no choice but to help the dead who came to her. One spirit had referred to her energy as a flare, or a fire in the sky. He told her that her abilities were visible to the dead from miles away. Even if she tried, she could not hide from them. If they needed help, they would follow her until she did her duty to them. She was no stranger to avoiding them like the plague, but they would only pacify her for so long before demanding her attention.

The dead following her in her waking hours were bad enough, but those who entered her sleep felt like a full-on assault. Instances of spirit-induced dreams, memory transfers she called them, had become more and more common, causing her sleep debt to reach debilitating levels. Although she used spirit memories to solve their murders, seeing their memories had proven to be traumatic for her.

Hazel had lost count of how many murders she had seen in her nightmares. How many corpses? How many lives being torn apart had she watched helplessly? But there was no way for her to stop them. Whether they were transferring their memories to her from next to her bed, or from another location altogether, she did not know. But they had found a way to infiltrate her mind, giving her no escape from their needs.

Emily's memories haunted her. Emily had a husband, Joshua, and a young daughter, Bella. Her family grieved for her. She had witnessed Bella's tears. Witnessed her begging for her mommy to come home. They did not know where she was for weeks, possibly longer, and now they would be told about her body's discovery in the swamp.

She knew little about the other victim, Malerie. Malerie's memories showed her the shack where she was held after her abduction, and even the swampy area where her body was discarded. Hazel did not know if Malerie had left behind a husband or children, but the guilt of having ignored Malerie when her spirit first reached out for help ate at Hazel's conscience.

She desperately wanted to help them, not just get them out of her head, but it would be impossible to manage another murder victim, much less two, if she kept her job at the Public

Defender's Office. Not knowing how she would pay her rent if she quit, she resigned to having to talk to her police officer boyfriend, Tate Cormier, about her options. Although they had not been romantically involved for long, her near decade long friendship with him had propelled their relationship forward to a more serious level than most people would have been in such a short time. She didn't like asking for help, but she would have to.

***

Time seemed to go in slow motion as Hazel waited for Tate to get off work. Candy's own spirit boyfriend, Jake, had arrived at their apartment, and left with Candy, as Hazel watched the clock tick. Jake's appearances had been irregular ever since his death because he still had trouble controlling his energy. So, Hazel did not complain when he could visit Candy, although sharing her best friend required some getting used to.

Candy, having been murdered a year prior, and Jake, having been murdered just over a month ago, had been in a relationship in life. They were both murdered by a woman named Harmony, who became obsessed with Jake and had killed Candy out of jealousy. The truth of Candy's murder was unknown to Jake, so he had gotten into a relationship with Harmony after Candy's murder, only to reject her once her psychotic behavior became apparent. Once he turned her away, the unstable Harmony killed him too.

Harmony got away with the murders for longer than she should have. She was an unassuming young woman who had only ever come across as the grieving girlfriend. After seeing Harmony in several of Jake's memory transfers, Hazel attempted to get close to the young woman, only to find herself, and Tate, fully enveloped in Harmony's obsessive tendencies.

Not long after Hazel met her, Harmony had focused her attention on Hazel's admittedly attractive boyfriend. Tate, being a police officer, used his connections to get Harmony arrested, but only after a near fatal standoff in the Carrolton Cemetery. Tate suffered a gunshot wound to his shoulder, but the police arrived before anything worse happened. Harmony was now sitting in a prison cell where she belonged.

After a few hours of flipping through television stations, Tate's familiar knock sounded at the door. A wide grin crawled across Hazel's previously passive face as she jumped off the sofa and ran to open the front door. Grabbing Tate by the collar of his police uniform, she pulled him through the threshold and into her lips. She could feel him smiling against her mouth as he dropped his bags on the kitchen table and wrapped his arms around her.

"Miss me?" he asked. His blue-gray eyes made her knees weak.

"Very much." Still on her tiptoes from the last kiss, her pulse quickened as she kissed him again.

"Good." Wrapping his arm around her shoulders, he guided her to the table, pulling out a chair for her to sit. "I brought Chinese food. Are you hungry?"

She smiled and nodded, leaning forward as he opened the bag and pulled out the food containers. "Thank you for always feeding me. I think I would starve without you."

He placed a container in front of her before taking his own seat. "Well, good thing I won't let that happen."

Hazel had not realized how ravenous she was until the food was in front of her. The smell was mouthwatering with all of its MSG-filled goodness. She often felt guilty about him always spending his money on takeout food for them, but she was completely inept at cooking. Thankfully, he seemed to love her anyway and didn't mind.

She hated to dampen the mood with mentions of the news, but she knew she needed to ask him about the murders. So, pulling off the metaphorical Band-aid, she brought up the conversation that was weighing on her mind.

"I saw they found two bodies in the Honey Island area."

Tate nodded, wiping his mouth with a napkin. "Yeah. There was a lot of talk about it around the precinct. Do you think the other body belongs to Emily?" Tate already knew the answer, but he asked anyway. Probably to open up the conversation he knew she needed to have but did not want to. She always worried about bringing up spirit obligations to him out of fear of overwhelming him, although he constantly assured her otherwise. Spirits were her obligation, but she didn't want them to be his as well.

During the first several years of her friendship with him, she kept her ability to communicate with the dead a secret from him. Once they had taken the leap into a romantic relationship, she no longer hid it from him. Spirits had a way of taking over her life, so her relationship with Tate could not last if she were leaving him in the dark. He did not appreciate the danger some spirits brought with them, however. The last spirit-led mystery had nearly gotten him killed, but he knew she had an obligation to help them. So, although her role sometimes scared him, he did his best to be a supportive boyfriend, no matter how worried it sometimes made him.

"Yes. I know they haven't released that information yet, but I know it's her. I don't know how I know, but I do." Her chest felt heavy, but she continued. "I feel terrible for her family. Her daughter is so young. It's just not fair. Any leads over who could have done this?"

He shook his head, sinking her heart. "Not yet... at least not that they are saying. It has all the hallmarks of a serial killer, though. I hope they catch the person before another woman gets taken."

"Yeah. I do too. I'm not looking forward to getting involved in another murder case, but I feel like I have no choice but to help these spirits if they come to me again. Malerie has already reached out to me once. I won't be able to ignore her indefinitely. Emily hasn't approached me yet, but she has invaded my dreams more than once. I'm sure I'll happen upon her sooner than later."

Tate nodded, but Hazel could tell he was not comfortable with the idea.

"I know you have to help them. I just wish murder victims would stop finding you for a while. I can't have you falling under the radar of another killer." His eyebrows drew together as he reached for her hand. "I don't want you approaching this murderer if you discover their identity. Please give new information to me. I'll get it to someone who will listen. Promise me. I need to keep you safe."

Hazel licked her lips as her stomach turned. He knew her too well. "I will. I don't want to end up in the sights of another killer, either. I really

don't even know how much time I can give to
these spirits. Although I realize it's not really my
decision. I just don't know how I'm going to help
both of them with my obligations at work."

Tate tilted his head, squeezing her hand
gently. "Have you ever thought about giving up
this apartment?"

Hazel chuckled. "I've got to live somewhere,
so no. I doubt I can find a better rate. Hauntings
save money." He knew it was true. Candy's
spiritual tantrums every time the realtor showed
the apartment to a potential tenant had earned
Hazel a huge discount for an apartment in
downtown New Orleans.

A smile crept across his face and Hazel raised
her eyebrows, unsure what he was getting at.

"You could move in with me. It's not like we
aren't together every night, anyway."

Hazel nearly choked on her Chinese. Sure, she
thought about moving in with Tate, but were
they really ready for that? They had been friends
since undergrad, but they had only been in a
romantic relationship for a few months. She had
stayed at his house for a few weeks when her
apartment lost power after Hurricane Ida, but

that was not meant to be permanent. She tried to lick her lips again, but her mouth had gone dry.

"Are you sure we're ready for that?"

He arched his eyebrow in the way that always made her blush.

"Why wouldn't we be? Are you not ready?"

"Oh, no. I didn't mean it like that. I want to be with you forever... I just didn't want to assume you were ready for that level of commitment with me. I'm kind of a mess."

Tate smirked before kissing her hand.

"I know who you are, Hazel Watson. And I've been by your side, anyway. I love you. That isn't going to change. After everything we've been through, that love has only grown."

Tate got out of his chair and dropped onto one knee, still holding Hazel's hand. She felt dizzy. Her mouth fell open, but she did not know what to say. Fumbling with his pocket, he pulled out a small velvet box. Her breath caught in her chest as her heart leaped.

"I wasn't going to do this in this way, but it is clear you need to hear this right now."

"Tate..." Her voice shook as she used her unoccupied hand to cover her mouth.

"Life offers many challenges. I know I can meet them if you're willing to face them with me. When I met you, I knew I'd met my match. It was only a matter of time until we arrived at this moment. I know you're the only one I want to share the rest of my life with. So... I guess what I'm asking is... will you marry me?"

He opened the box, revealing a sparkling stone encased in white gold. Her trembling hand remained in his grasp, but she could not speak. Tears fell as he looked at her expectantly.

"Hazel? Are you in there?"

The sound of his voice pulled her into the present. She nodded her head enthusiastically.

"Is that a yes?"

"Yes... yes," she cried, falling into one of his famous bear hugs. Her body shook with the force of her sobs, but it was happy tears. The sort of tears she hadn't had in a very long time.

"Phew!" Tate said as he pretended to wipe sweat from his brow. She steadied her hand as he slid the ring on her finger. She stared at it for a while, almost as though she were waiting for it to disappear and for her to wake up. But it was not a dream. She was engaged.

When they went to bed that night, it was like they could not get enough of each other. They made love with an insatiable passion. With none of their previously held reservations, those saying she wasn't good enough. She let herself drink him in, becoming completely intoxicated. The spicy, woodsy, citrus blend of his cologne filled her nose. The strength and hardness of his body pulsed against her. The salty taste of sweat on his skin. Her body swam with ecstasy. The rest of the world drifted away, leaving only the two of them. She did not think about her stressful job, or the murder victims who wanted to pull her into their worlds. All she thought about that night was the love of her life who was in her bed.

2

Room for Three

Sitting at a tiny pink and white table, the little girl with chestnut pigtails drew a picture of her family with crayons. The mommy, daddy and daughter stood outside, in front of a swing set, smiling brightly. She sang to herself softly, a blend of humming and nursery rhymes. Her tune changed as she added thick trees in the background of the picture. It became darker. Yellow eyes were colored in, peeking through the trees. Dropping her crayon and stopping her song, she wrote the words 'I see you' before the scene went dark.

***

"Show me!" Candy squealed. She bounced up and down as though she had a corporeal form. "I'm so excited!"

Hazel blushed as she reached her left hand out to Candy, who took it excitedly.

"It's so pretty!"

"Thanks. I'm still a bit shocked."

Candy shot Hazel a sideways glance.

"As if. We all knew it was coming, eventually. Maybe not this soon, but it was inevitable."

Hazel smiled as her heart sank, just a bit. She still hadn't told Candy about her and Tate's decision to give up her apartment and move in together. Scenes from her strange dream had filled her mind that morning, so she had admittedly not thought about it. Although she knew Candy's history in that apartment was a nightmare, she did not know how Candy would feel about leaving it, or if she even would leave it.

Hazel had not known Candy in life. She met Candy when moving into their apartment about a year prior. Candy haunted that apartment ever since she was murdered there, nearly a year before Hazel had moved in. Although she met the end of her life there, she never seemed willing to give up her home, using relentless tactics to scare away potential tenants. It was how their friendship began.

Hazel cleared her throat. There was no use in waiting to tell her.

"There's something else I needed to talk to you about."

Candy's eyes narrowed, but she still smiled. "Are you pregnant?"

A laugh escaped Hazel's throat. "No way!"

Candy's face fell into a frown. "I was about to get excited. Well then, what do you want to talk about?"

Hazel hesitated, hoping Candy would be okay with their decision to leave the apartment, but she was scared to tell her. "It's about the apartment... Tate and I have decided to give it up so I can quit my miserable job. He wants me to move in with him."

She braced for Candy's response. "Oh." Candy pressed her lips together before glancing around the room.

"I guess I expected that to happen one day as well."

She looked up to meet Hazel's eyes, smiling slightly, but Hazel's heart was heavy.

"Candy... I'm..."

"It's okay, Hazel. I'm okay. It's time for me to give up this place. It served its purpose when it led me to you."

Candy reached out and took Hazel's hands, rubbing her knuckles gently. Hazel's emotions bubbled just below the surface. Even though Candy was a spirit, she always felt solid to Hazel, which only made her long for Candy's life more. She had never felt her friend's hands when they were warm.

"I'm content with us leaving this apartment... together."

Although her eyes glistened with tears, Hazel smiled. "You'll come with me?"

"I told you I'm your ride or die, doll. Of course, I'll come with you. You don't think Tate will mind you making his house haunted?"

Hazel grimaced, but let out a chuckle. "Oh, gosh... I don't know if he's even considered it like that." She narrowed her eyes at Candy. "We will need some ground rules, though."

Candy joined Hazel in giggles, playfully smacking Hazel on the arm. "I've never been much for rules."

"Tough."

***

When Tate returned to Hazel's apartment that night, she felt a tad bit out of place. They were engaged, but she was still stunned by it. It was only a few months since she was fighting with herself about making a move on him, unsure if he wanted to be more than friends. Their romantic relationship had moved so fast, but they had been friends for the better part of a decade, so had it really? He said no, and she knew she could not imagine loving him much more than she did, so what would be fast for other couples did not seem too fast for them. When she answered the door and saw him in the corridor, the smile on his lips was reflected in his eyes. It told her all she needed to know about their relationship. He loved her. He wanted her.

She was good enough, no matter how much her dismal self-esteem argued the fact.

"Hey there," he said as he pulled her into a kiss. She surrendered control of herself to his embrace.

"Hey to you."

They entered her apartment arm in arm. Candy had still been sitting on the sofa when he arrived, but she was gone by the time Hazel looked back for her. They had an understanding about giving each other space when their love interests were present, something they would not have to do once they moved into Tate's three-bedroom house because they would each have their own space.

"I missed you today. Well... I miss you every day." Tate smiled sheepishly, causing Hazel to blush.

He is so damn handsome.

"I missed you too. Oh... I told Candy about the move and she was excited. She did not seem to be against leaving the apartment."

Tate wrapped his arm around her waist and squeezed her gently. "That's great news. Is she here now?"

Tate looked around as though he could see Candy if she had been there, although he did not have the ability to see her. Hazel chuckled. It was something he always did, although he always came up with the same result.

"No. She left when you got here to give us privacy."

He abandoned his search for Candy's spirit and set his eyes back on Hazel. His face fell into a slight frown.

"It'll be good when she doesn't feel the need to leave just because I'm here. At least she will have her own space at my place. Did you tell her that?"

"I did. I think that will work out nicely. It'll be nice to know where she is more often. I feel like I don't see her as much as I used to, but I guess that's to be expected with me having you and her having Jake. I'm happy that both of us have a man... I just miss her is all."

Tate pulled her into a hug and kissed the top of her head. "Well, we will make sure she knows she is always welcome at the new house. I don't ever want her to feel like a third wheel."

Hazel nodded as she rose on her tiptoes to kiss

him. He was so much taller than her. He moaned softly into her lips.

"What was that for?"

"I told you I missed you..."

***

Leaving her bedroom later that night, Hazel scanned her apartment for Candy but did not see her.

Out on the town with Jake, I guess...

Even after death, Candy seemed to really like being around other people, something Hazel would never understand. Just the thought of running around the city nearly gave her hives. She went to the refrigerator to get more water out of the purification pitcher and shut off the lights to return to bed. Tate was in the shower, and her eyes were finding the fight to stay open difficult. Turning around from the light of the refrigerator, the sight in front of her caused her to lose the grip on her glass, dropping it to the floor. Water splashed across the kitchen. She was too caught up in the sight before her to be thankful the glass was plastic.

A woman, fairly translucent from her recent

death, stood in front of her. Her eyes were a bright blue, not unlike Candy's, and her hair was a deep chestnut. Hazel had never seen her before in life, but she had seen her daughter, who looked so much like her. She recognized the woman immediately.

"Emily," she gasped. "Emily Landry?"

The spirit, taken aback by Hazel's recognition of her, remained quiet as her eyes grew larger. After a few awkward moments of staring at each other, Emily nodded briskly. Her eyes darted around Hazel's apartment as though she did not know where she was or how she had gotten there. Feeling the water still dripping down her leg from the dropped glass, Hazel grabbed a towel on the counter and squatted down to clean the mess, while simultaneously trying to keep her eyes set on the spirit. Emily's emotions poured into the room like a steam engine, infiltrating Hazel's pores while she stood powerless to stop it. her hands trembled as she tried to wipe up the water she spilled. Irregular heartbeats made her dizzy, forcing her to drop the towel.

"You can speak to me, Emily. I can hear you. Please... tell me how I can help you."

Hazel's voice seemed to bring Emily's mind back to the present. She lowered herself to meet Hazel's eye. "I don't know how you can help me," Emily said in a shaky voice.

"Do you know who did this to you?" Hazel's heart fell under its own weight. She had asked that same question to so many people.

Emily shook her head and her emotions appeared to be bursting through. A single tear sparkled down her cheek.

"He wore a mask. I never saw his face. My daughter... my husband... what will they do?" Emily's hands trembled as she tried to pull the hair from her face.

Hazel looked to the floor as she fought Emily's emotions that bombarded her senses, threatening to take over her own.

"I don't know, but they're strong. I've seen them through your memories. Your daughter is resilient. She's special."

Hazel thought about Emily's daughter, Bella. When Hazel had seen her through Emily's memories, she could swear the little girl knew she was there, especially after her most recent dream. She wondered if Emily's daughter had otherworldly abilities. It sent a stab into her heart. She remembered what it was like to be a small child with such abilities, and it was not easy. There were so many moments where she had been filled with such terror, so many moments where she wished the spirits would leave her alone. She still felt that way sometimes, and she did not want this lively little girl to go through what she went through.

Emily smiled. "Yes. She is special."

The door creaked, causing both women to turn their heads in the direction of Hazel's bedroom. Tate popped his head out of the opening. His hair was still wet from the shower.

"Are you okay, love?" he asked before noticing Hazel stooped on the floor over a puddle of water. "Oh, no. What happened?" He rushed out to help her with a towel around his waist.

Emily's spirit vanished as Tate ran past her. Hazel, no longer distracted by the spirit in front of her, stared down at the puddle on the floor which was still wetting her feet.

"Oh, I dropped my glass. It's okay. I've got it."

She began mopping the water up with the towel as Tate grabbed a handful of paper napkins and kneeled down to help her. She looked him over as he kneeled close to her.

"You'd better watch out or you'll lose that towel around your waist."

He smirked, wiping up a large puddle of water near the table. "As long as Candy isn't here, then I think I'll be okay. I wouldn't want to give her a show."

Hazel laughed, instinctively glancing around for her best friend. "Oh, but she would hide herself if she were here and thought that was a possibility."

Tate checked to see that the towel was secure before leaning forward to mop up water that had splashed in a different spot on the floor.

"There," he said as he rose back to his feet and reached out a hand for Hazel. "We cleaned it together. Are you ready to take a shower?"

She looked down at the water still dripping from her leg, wiping it with the drenched towel in her hand. "Looks like I already did."

He chuckled as he refilled her glass of water and led her back to the bedroom.

3

Monsters
and Moving

"Joshua," she cried, her voice trembling. "I know what I saw! I know it sounds ridiculous, but I saw the Honey Island swamp monster, or something like it. It wasn't a man!"

Joshua's eyes narrowed. He did not believe her. She felt herself near her boiling point.

"Emily, you probably saw a hunter dressed in their hunting gear. There's no such thing as a swamp monster. It's just a tale parents tell their kids to make them stay out of the swamp. It's not real."

He reached forward and tried to hug her, but she pulled back. Her anger rose the more he doubted her.

"A seven-foot-tall hunter?" The tone of her voice was as serious as she could muster.

Joshua scoffed, shaking his head. "Look... I'm not saying you didn't see someone. I'm just saying it wasn't a monster. I'm sure there are plenty of tall hunters out there. Come on... I love you. It'll be okay."

He reached out to hug her again, but she crossed her arms across her chest like a truculent child. Her nostrils flared as heat poured through her body but her husband's smile began to cut through her annoyance.

"They're not even supposed to hunt near here. If they were, we should report it."

Joshua nodded. "I can do that. It's going to be okay."

She felt her annoyance retreat completely as she gazed into his blue eyes. She was still concerned about the figure she had seen across the canal, but she could not resist the handsome face of her loving husband. He reached out his arms one more time to hold her, and she obliged.

***

Hazel awoke more confused than traumatized, both of which common reactions to the spirit memories that often plagued her sleep. She was not surprised to have one of Emily's memories find their way into her unconscious mind after coming face to face with the spirit in her kitchen the night before. She searched the bedroom, hoping the woman was not somewhere lurking, thankful when she saw no one but Tate sleeping next to her. She wanted to see Emily's spirit because she wanted to help her, but she would rather not see her standing at the foot of her bed. Angela's appearance next to her bed months earlier still had her scared of the dark, even with her lifetime of seeing spirits.

She did not know what she could pull from the memory that was helpful, however. So, Emily saw something in the woods... a swamp monster she called it. Such things did not exist, or did they? Hazel realized she was the last person who could discount supernatural occurrences, but the thought of swamp monsters freaked her out. She grimaced, shaking the image from her mind and turning to watch Tate sleep. She hoped the peacefulness of his gentle breathing would calm her.

His eyes were no longer closed when she

turned to face him, however. She did not know how long he had been awake, but his goofy grin told her he had been watching her for a bit.

"What's with that face?" she said as she smirked back at him.

He chuckled. "You make very animated faces when you're thinking. It makes me wonder what's in that beautiful mind of yours."

He leaned over and kissed her. Warmth flooded her face.

"You do not want to know."

"I always want to know what you're thinking about... unless you think you don't love me anymore... I may not want to know that."

"Awe." She sighed as she moved closer to him. "That's too bad."

He arched an eyebrow at her and huffed. "Hey!"

She kissed him on the cheek and laughed. "I'm joking. I'm joking."

Groaning, he wrapped his arms around her and squeezed her gently. "I know. So am I. I'd even want to know that, although I hope it never happens."

She gazed up at him, adoration in her eyes. "It won't."

"Good. So, we didn't talk about what you want to do with your job and when you want to move in with me. I am assuming those things need to happen simultaneously."

Hazel nodded, although she did not yet have a legitimate plan for leaving her job. She just knew she needed to. "Yea... I guess since Emily's spirit showed up in my kitchen last night... I should probably get on that."

Tate eyed her warily, slightly pulling back so he could look into her eyes. "Wait... is that why you dropped that glass of water? Emily was here in the apartment?"

Hazel nodded begrudgingly. She hated even admitting it out of fear that one more ghost would cause him to change his mind about her moving in with him.

"Damn," he said, pulling her back into the crook of his arm and kissing the top of her head. "I guess it was only a matter of time before she came to you, though. Right?"

"Yeah. I expected her to show up eventually

because I've already seen her memories a few times. I figured she was around."

Fiddling with her fingernails nervously, she was unsure if leaving her job was the right thing to do. Crippling self-doubt was her dark passenger. She knew she could not continue on the same path she was on, though. The spirits did not leave her much time to do her job, especially if she included all the spirits she avoided when she should not. Having spent so many years in school to be an attorney, she knew it was a waste, but she also knew the career path really was not for her. It caused her more stress than anything. Not to mention, her attorney father and two attorney brothers back in New Mexico would be disappointed. It would reinforce her black sheep status in the family.

"Did she tell you anything? Anything helpful, I mean. Something that could help to catch her killer?"

Hazel shrugged weakly. "Unfortunately, no. She mostly just cried about her family before you walked in. She disappeared when she saw you."

"Oh, I'm sorry about that. I heard the glass clatter and thought you were hurt."

Hazel reached over to caress his arm. He relaxed into her touch.

"It's not your fault, babe. You didn't know she was there. I did dream about her last night, another memory. She was telling her husband about a creature she saw in the swamp near her house. She called it a swamp monster. Said it was seven feet tall. Her husband didn't believe her and insisted it was a hunter dressed in gear to camouflage himself. I don't know what to think. She was really afraid of it, whatever it was."

Tate pursed his lips. "Hmm... like the Honey Island Swamp Monster?"

"Do you mean it's a real thing? Is it different from the Rougarou?" Hazel's voice was incredulous. She could not believe there was a real seven-foot-tall creature out there with a legend about it, although she had briefly heard about the Rougarou, another Louisiana cryptid. The hair on her arms stood up at the thought of it.

"I know the Honey Island Swamp Monster is a real legend, but I doubt it's an actual creature. I think it's similar to the Rougarou. Some of these stories go back to the time when there were mostly Native Americans in this area, but I've only ever heard the stories. There have been many reports of this sort of thing, though. I guess stranger things exist, so it's possible."

She sighed. "Great. I already deal with ghosts and now you're telling me that I have to deal with possible swamp monsters?"

Tate chuckled and wrapped his arms all the way around her, pulling her on top of him, and wrapping his legs around her like she was wrapped in a pretzel. "I'll protect you by keeping you in my Kung Fu grip... see... no one can get to you now."

Hazel burst into laughter although Tate tried to maintain his serious protector face, only making her laugh more. She laid on top of him, wrapped in his arms and legs, as she laughed into his chest.

"Okay! I get it, but I can't breathe. You can let me go already!"

He grunted, looking at her as though she had said something ridiculous. "No way. You expect me to let you go so the swamp monster can get you? No way. You can't make me do it. You're going to just have to walk around like this. I must keep you safe. I've told you this."

She did not know how he was keeping a straight face, but she was laughing so much she almost peed on herself. Instead of continuing to struggle, she started kissing his neck. He moaned as his grip on her loosened. It did not take long for his body to get excited enough for him to unwrap his legs from around her legs so he could get into a more convenient position to progress the ever-developing moment of intimacy that had started out with a pretzel hold and a laugh fest.

Before Hazel knew it, he had flipped her back over and it was her legs wrapped around him instead, but he was not struggling to get free.

"We will get nothing done if you keep kissing me on the neck in the mornings, afternoons, and evenings," he said as he kissed her across her face with each word. She felt herself growing hot and knew he could see it in her face.

Pulling his face to hers, she kissed him deeply on the mouth before saying, "then I guess we won't get anything done."

He chuckled as he kept kissing her. Melting

into his touch, she felt herself become intoxicated by it, as though the high it gave her elevated her to a higher level of existence. Her eyes rolled back as he kissed a trail down her body.

When she finally climbed out of bed, her head felt like it was floating. She had to sit back down and let the sensation calm down before she dared walk around the room. Tate leaned over her back and wrapped his arms around her.

"Are you going to make it? Or do you want to just come and lie back down with me?"

"I want to lie down with you all day, but I am quite hungry. Should we get something to eat?"

Her stomach growled loudly, and they both snickered.

"Yeah... I guess I should probably feed you then. Do you want to walk over to that little café around the block, or should I order something for delivery?"

"We can go for a walk, since it looks like the rain has stopped. I may die if I don't eat soon."

Hazel stood up successfully and began digging for a clean outfit to put on. One thing she would be happy about when moving into Tate's house was having her own washing machine and dryer. She was definitely tired of never having clean clothes because the washer and dryer in her apartment complex were on another floor and were shared by other tenants. She hated doing laundry there, so she usually only ever had about ten percent of her wardrobe clean at any given time. Tate followed her out of the bed and pulled on his pants that were draped over the desk chair. She stopped what she was doing, just for a moment, to ogle at him.

"Damn, you're so hot. Did I ever tell you that?" She blushed, not believing herself capable of saying such a thing. Her shyness around him seemed to go away with the weight of the new diamond ring on her finger.

He looked at her with a mischievous smile. "Actually, I don't think you've ever said that to me, so thank you. I think you're pretty gorgeous yourself."

Making a face somewhere between a smile and a grimace, she brushed her hair. "Well, now you know what has been on my mind for a really long time. You said you wanted to know what

I'm thinking. And thank you, but I'm nothing special."

He closed the distance between them and dipped her back into a movie style kiss. "You're very special and exquisite. And you're mine. I'm the luckiest man in the world."

"You, sir, are just trying to butter me up so I'll get back in bed with you, but I can't do that because I'm going to literally die if I don't eat five minutes ago, so let's go."

"Who are you and what have you done with Hazel?" Tate asked as he chuckled, opening the door for them to leave the bedroom and go for breakfast. "Well, whoever you are, let's get you fed so I can get you back to bed."

Hazel stuck her tongue out at him before walking out of the apartment. He was right; she did not know what had come over her since he proposed to her the day before, but she liked how freeing it felt to no longer be so shy around him. She guessed, while she was feeling so bold, she should contact her office about taking some time off before she lost her nerve.

***

The sun was shining as they exited the building, but there were still small puddles on the ground. They avoided them as they traversed the broken concrete on their way to a small cafe a block away. As was typical in New Orleans, the sound of traffic and the smell of nearby garage greeted them along their way. It made her miss her parents' ranch, where there was more nature and less evidence of people.

After their late breakfast, Hazel called her office to put in for unpaid leave while she coped with her post-traumatic stress disorder, or at least that was what she told them. She had developed post-traumatic stress disorder months earlier after being abducted and nearly killed. The entire incident was traumatic, but having to kill him in self-defense was what had affected Hazel the most. She experienced many symptoms of PTSD over the past few months, but it is not the real reason she was leaving her job, although she couldn't tell them that.

Needing to vacate her apartment before the next rent was due, she and Tate also decided to move her into his house within the week. She had met her year lease and was now on a month-to-month plan, which caused an increase in her rent. Money was going to get increasingly tight, but she needed time to figure things out.

Once they got back to her apartment and she finished her phone call, they climbed into Tate's car and drove to find some moving boxes and tape so she could get her apartment packed up. The plan was for her to start packing, and then he would help her when he got back from his shift. Her apartment was small, so she knew it would not take her all that long to get all of her belongings into boxes.

So, as Tate got ready to go to work, she began going through her belongings and getting them into somewhat organized piles. She wanted to be able to find everything once the boxes were brought to Tate's house so she could unpack them quickly. She did not want to live in boxes while trying to figure out where to put everything.

Hazel packed her apartment with a sense of nostalgia. Her life had not been especially happy in the apartment, aside from the girl's nights with Candy and the memories she had built with Tate, but it was her first actual home as an adult, and that made it special. Candy did not have her own belongings to pack, so she oversaw the process, much to Hazel's annoyance, because she could be rather bossy.

When Tate returned to her apartment after his shift, he would do the heavy lifting to get her belongings to his house. She was not particularly looking forward to the commute, since Tate lived twenty minutes outside of the city, but with her taking leave from her job at the Public Defender's Office, so she would not have to brave the New Orleans traffic regularly.

Something Candy was excited about was that she would finally have her own space again. That way, she would no longer need to leave whenever Hazel and Tate needed alone time. With Tate's home having three bedrooms, it was a luxury they could afford. Plus, with Candy's spirit boyfriend still being on their side of the veil, they could also use alone time together.

Deciding to wait and do her dirty laundry at Tate's house that night, she bagged it up and packed the clean clothes into her suitcase before bringing a few things down to her car.

Stumbling to her car with two boxes precariously stacked on top of each other, something blocked her path, causing both boxes to topple to the ground. She lifted startled eyes, landing them on the familiar form in front of her. She had expected to see a living person, someone with the corporeal mass to create the impact she suffered, but it was not a living person at all.

Long, dark hair and exotic amber eyes loomed in front of her. The spirit of Malerie Ledet held a fire in her expression, a determination to be seen. Hazel ignored her before, but it was clear she would no longer take no for an answer. Hazel stood there, dumbfounded, unsure how to proceed.

Bending over to pick up the fallen boxes, she whispered just over her breath. "To my car."

The spirit nodded and glided alongside her, appearing in the passenger side of the car before Hazel had even dropped the boxes into her trunk. Checking to see that no one else was nearby, Hazel slipped into her car, setting her phone onto the dashboard to appear as though she were simply on a call. Malerie sat patiently, seeming to be relieved to finally have Hazel's attention.

"I'm sorry for not talking to you weeks ago, but I know who you are. I was under a lot of pressure then, although I realize it doesn't seem like much of an excuse. You're Malerie Ledet... right?"

The woman nodded, turning to meet Hazel's eyes. Hazel shuddered from the chill of the spirit's presence as much as from the look in Malerie's eyes.

"Do you know who did this to you?"

Malerie shook her head slowly, dropping her eyes to her hands. Deep, dark cuts scarred Malerie's flesh, possibly from the fight for her life. She balled up her fists in her lap.

"He's going to take another," Malerie said. Her voice was fuzzy, as though it was coming out of a short-wave radio.

"Another woman? Do you know who?"

Hazel's heart felt heavy with urgency, but she did not know how to fulfill whatever duty the universe expected from her. Rubbing her temples with her hands, she squeezed her eyes shut, hoping a solution would come to her.

"No. He hunts for them. She'll fall into his lap, and she won't know he's there until it's too late."

Just as her words landed, the spirit of Malerie Ledet disappeared, leaving Hazel alone in her car with a heavier weight on her shoulders than she had that morning. Pulling herself together as best as she could, she climbed out of her car and walked back to her apartment.

Tate already had a kitchen full of pots, pans, dishes and utensils, but she had some items she wanted to keep, so they would just have two of everything. She wrapped everything that was breakable into newspaper and tried to not make the boxes too heavy, although she knew Tate would carry them two at a time, regardless. Making herself a sandwich for lunch before packing up the kitchen, Hazel scanned her nearly completely packed apartment. Although they planned for days of packing, she had done it in one.

She gazed around her small kitchen for what would be one of the last times she would see it. She thought back to her first visit to the apartment when she first met Candy. That moment had been so important in her life. Seeing Candy on the sofa, Hazel left the opened box in the kitchen and joined her.

"What are you up to, Candy? Are you still okay with us moving?"

Candy looked over at her and smiled. "Of course, I am, doll. I think I'm actually a bit excited about it. It'll be pretty cool to have my own room. I'll have to show Jake where my room is, so he knows where to find me after today. I wouldn't want him popping in on you two lovebirds." Hazel rolled her eyes, but Candy did not take the bait. "You are spending the night at Tate's tonight, right?"

"Yeah. He's going to come grab these boxes when he gets off and we'll go back to his place. You can always stay here tonight if you want, though... if you're not ready to go yet."

"I'll think about it, but I think I'd rather just go when you go, if that's okay."

Hazel reached out and placed her hand on Candy's arm.

"Of course, that's okay. It's going to be your home, too. You even have a television in your bedroom, so you can watch your favorite murder mystery shows, even when we are watching something else. I think it's going to be great. I'm excited too. I've been missing you lately since you've been away from home a lot. I look forward to having you back home more. You and Jake will be able to be together and Tate and I will be together, and we can give each other the space we need but still have access to each other as well. Tate is happy about being able to give you a room for yourself, so don't think you're intruding or anything like that. It's your home too. You're stuck with us."

"Yuck," Candy said playfully. "So, how much packing do you have left to do?"

Hazel glanced into the kitchen, eyeing the open cabinets and their lack of contents.

"Not that much, actually. I'm nearly done. It's not like I have much stuff." Hazel rose back to her feet. "I guess I will get it done now, before Tate gets here."

***

Tate arrived just after 6 p.m. with veggie burgers from a restaurant they liked a few blocks away.

She would miss some of the nearby restaurants, but she would enjoy more of Tate's cooking. He was certainly a better cook than she was.

"Wow!" Tate said as he glanced around her apartment and saw all the boxes. "You got a lot done today. That's great!"

"Thanks!" She kissed him and pulled their burgers out of the bag. "I actually got everything packed and am ready to go. I didn't want to keep you up too late helping me pack, especially with us having to make the trip back to your house afterwards."

He gazed into her eyes before biting into his sandwich.

"You seem like you're in a great mood. I was worried you would be sad to leave your place."

She finished chewing the food in her mouth before smiling and responding. "I'm not sad at all. I'm actually feeling excited, as is Candy. We are both looking forward to the new arrangement and moving out of the place where we went through so much shit. We can create better memories in the new house. Having you and Jake will only make that more likely."

He smiled as he chewed, reaching his foot out under the table to rub hers.

"We will definitely create wonderful memories there."

"Excuse me, sir, but I think you're playing footsie with me."

"I am," he said, winking playfully.

"Get a room!" Candy yelled from the living room, causing Hazel to laugh and almost spit out her food.

"We will have one in about an hour," she yelled back. Tate watched the one-sided conversation in confusion. He did not know what Candy was saying, so it looked like Hazel was talking to herself.

"What are y'all talking about?"

"Oh," Hazel giggled. "She yelled at us to get a room."

Tate laughed before yelling out to Candy as well, "We've already got one!"

Candy looked towards him and laughed before turning to talk to Hazel. She wagged her finger at Hazel as though she were a naughty child. "You're changing... you're becoming more outgoing around him. I like it. I'm proud of you.

I don't know if it's all the manly lovin' you've been getting, or if it's the new diamond ring on your finger, but I like it. Keep it up."

"Uh... thanks... I think."

"So," Tate interrupted, as he threw his burger in the trash. "Are you ready to pack up the cars?"

"Definitely. I'm getting tired, so the sooner we can get all of this where it goes, the sooner I can shower and climb into bed."

"Sooner you can climb into bed with me... yeah, let's rush this process then." He wiggled his eyebrows at her before grabbing a box and stacking it on top of another. Just as Hazel suspected, he would stack as many boxes as possible to make fewer trips, which made her glad she did not overfill them.

***

They were able to fit most of Hazel's boxes within both of their cars. There were still a few pieces of furniture and random items they would have to pick up later, but she had everything she needed to be comfortable at his house that night. She breathed a sigh of relief.

Following Tate on the way back to his house

in her own car, she fought to keep her eyes open while she drove. The sun was down, making her struggle even more difficult. The traffic to leave the city after rush hour was a little lighter than it would have been a few hours earlier, taking less than thirty minutes to get there. Thankfully, Candy's incessant talking did its job of keeping her awake. Pulling her car into one side of the garage, she felt giddy. She was home, her new home, the home she would share with Tate. They were getting married. It was all wonderful changes, and that was a relief.

Before she grabbed her stuff from the passenger seat and opened her own door, Tate had already walked around and opened the door for her.

"Are you ready to go inside, my future bride?"

She blushed, taking his hand and letting him help her out of the car. "Yes. Let's do this."

She went to open the trunk and grab boxes, but Tate stopped her, hooked his arms underneath her legs, and picked her up so he was carrying her. "I'll get the boxes for you, love. I'm going to get you inside so you can go take a relaxing bath. I know you're exhausted."

A goofy grin crossed Hazel's face as he carried her across the garage and then over the threshold into the house. Candy chuckled behind them, but she went in the other direction when they crossed into the master bedroom. Hazel was not sure where she had gone, but she figured Candy probably went to watch television, or look for her new bedroom. He carried her all the way into the master bathroom before setting her down. Reaching over, he turned on the faucet for the tub and kissed her gently.

"Now, you relax. I'll get a glass of wine for you, then I'll take the boxes out. I'll come back to check on you."

"You're too good to me. You're going to turn me into a spoiled brat if you keep it up."

"I'll take my chances. I'll be back."

He left, shutting the door behind him.

The warm water felt good on her sore body. She always took a shower in her apartment, but she thought she could get used to having a garden tub now that she had more time to spend in it. Tate had dropped off a glass of wine and stole a kiss before leaving the bathroom to grab the boxes out of their vehicles. The spoiling almost made Hazel feel like she was in a fantasy world, but it was not a fantasy. It was real.

4

A New
Space

Hazel's first night officially living with Tate was
surreal. She could have never imagined, even six
months ago, that she would end up engaged to
Tate and living in his home. Candy had her own
room, so she was excited to no longer have to
send her best friend out of the house for her
and Tate to have alone time. They would each
have their own space, but Candy would always
be nearby, at least when she was not out on the
town. As soon as Tate left for work on her first

full day living in the new place, she knocked on Candy's door and found her friend lying on the bed. Hazel entered the room and hopped onto Candy's bed to join her.

"So... how do you like having your own room?"

Candy looked up at her, but Hazel noticed something unexpected in her eyes. She expected to see some sadness after leaving an apartment that held so many memories, but Hazel felt like there was something more bothering Candy.

"It's nice." The positive words did not match the emotion hidden in Candy's eyes.

"What's wrong, Candy? Is there something I can get for you... something to make it homier for you?"

Candy hesitated, threading her fingers through her extensively long red locks.

"I would like my stuff that was not in the apartment... the stuff in my storage unit... If it's still there."

Hazel's eyes widened as her eyebrows lifted. "You have a storage unit?"

Candy nodded. "I did. My friend Hera put my belongings into a storage unit after everything happened. My family couldn't be bothered to deal with my stuff."

Candy's eyes shot downward. She had never brought up her family before, but Hazel always thought it was just because she missed them, not because they had abandoned her in death. Hazel could not imagine why Candy's family did not arrange to gather her belongings after she died, but she could see why it was upsetting to her best friend.

"Is Hera in the city?"

"She was last time I saw her, but that was at least a year ago. There's a chance she has moved, but she always loved the city, so I can't imagine her leaving. She's probably on Facebook or something."

Hazel reached out to hold Candy's hands. Her heart broke for her friend.

"I'll find her. Do you think she'd believe me if I told her about you?"

Candy's eyes looked up expectantly. Hazel could tell it was not a possibility she had considered.

"She might. You would do that for me? Expose yourself? I didn't want to ask."

"Of course, I would. I just hope it would help me get into your storage unit. I'm a perfect stranger, so I don't think she'd give me your belongings otherwise."

Candy nodded. "Yeah, I considered that. I hope we can get my stuff, though. Some of that stuff is important to me, but I never had a way to get it before I met you. And we didn't have space for anything in the apartment, but I figured, now that I have my own space, I can have my stuff back."

Hazel gently squeezed the icy hands in her grasp, willing the warmth to return to them.

"We'll find a way. I promise."

***

Opening her laptop and watching it come to life, Hazel thought about her task at hand. She had met none of Candy's friends or family, and she was admittedly nervous about it. What if Hera did not believe her and slammed the door in her face? How would she even convince her? She had approached the family members of spirits so many times before, but this was different. Candy meant the world to her, and she was scared to screw it up.

Typing Hera's full name into the social media search engine, she watched as smiling faces populated on the screen. Blanchard was a common Cajun last name, but Hera was not a common first name, so it did not take long to find Candy's friend.

"That's her!" Candy squealed, leaning her head over Hazel's lap to get a closer look at the face on the screen. "Awe! She looks so pretty! And her hair is still purple... Why am I not surprised?"

Hazel felt a slight tinge of jealousy, or some other emotion she could not place, but she bit it back. She had been the only friend in Candy's life ever since she met her, and it was hard to think of the time before her best friend was murdered. She longed to have known Candy in life, but she had no way of making that happen. She clicked on the profile, expanding Hera's life across the screen.

Candy was right, Hera was pretty. Her short hair was colored in a pastel purple with streaks of aqua and pink, and her skin had a similar porcelain appearance to that of Candy's. Her profile said she was engaged to a woman named Adele Breaux and was working as a social worker with victims of domestic abuse. Hazel wondered if that career choice was motivated by Candy's murder. Hazel's stomach sank thinking about it.

Candy leaned back against the headboard and cupped her face in her hands. "Awe... I miss her. She's engaged like you! Both of my best friends are getting married. That's amazing."

Her words sounded happy, but her tone revealed other emotions. Hazel's heart tightened in her chest. Candy could never get married or be a mom. She wondered if that was the thought going through Candy's mind when she acknowledged the engagements of her two closest friends. It almost made Hazel feel guilty for her own progressing life when Candy was stuck in time.

Adding Hera as a friend, she hoped Candy's friend would accept the friend's request. Not being big on social media, Hazel only had a basic account which would allow her to search through profiles, but she had little about herself on the platform. Realizing Hera may not follow her back if her profile looked like it belonged to a bot, she added a few basic details about herself, as well as a few pictures. Adding anything about herself onto the platform made her uncomfortable, but it was for a good cause, so she did it anyway.

Hera must have been online because Hazel received a confirmation of her friend's request within only a few minutes. Candy noticed it first, shooting upright on the bed and pointing excitedly at the laptop screen.

"Look! She followed you back!" Candy popped up on her knees and bounced up and down enthusiastically. Hazel hesitantly opened Hera's profile back up and stared at the notification, confirming they were now friends. She did not know what to do next. She looked to Candy for guidance.

"Now what?"

"Message her!"

"And tell her what? What if I scare her off?"

Candy bit her lip. Her bouncing simmered down, and she sat on the bed, staring at the screen.

"What if you ask to speak to her in person?

Tell her it's about me. Maybe introduce yourself as an attorney working on my case. She won't know you left your job."

Nodding, Hazel dropped her fingers to the keyboard and typed the message. She proposed meeting at a coffee shop to discuss Candy's case. Her stomach felt like it was filled with buzzing bees. She knew she only had one chance to prove to Hera that Candy was still around, but she also knew most people would not believe her claims. She hoped Hera was as open-minded as Tate. It was the only way she could get Candy's belongings out of storage.

Her message remained unread for several agonizing minutes. Just as she almost lost hope and closed the laptop, she received a response from Hera.

"When?" was all it said. Hazel's heart nearly leaped out of her chest as she typed her response. One day, until she would need to convince Hera to turn over Candy's belongings to her with the claim that Candy's spirit remained on earth and wanted them. She did not dare to give herself over one day out of fear that she would chicken out.

She and Candy spoke extensively about how to approach the meeting with Hera, but ultimately agreed to speak honestly with her. Candy really believed Hera was open-minded enough to believe she was still around. They planned to share some tidbits that only Candy would know, and hope it would prove her ghostly existence to her friend. They did not have a plan for if it did not work, but that was their usual way of going about things. Their plans rarely worked out, anyway.

***

Hazel was excited to see Tate when he got home from his shift that night. He still gave her butterflies in her belly, and she hoped that sensation would never cease to happen when he was near her. In the living world, Tate was her best friend. She still had to pinch herself to believe they were engaged. It was never an outcome she pictured for her life, but she could not imagine it any differently now that it was set in motion.

Walking into the house, Tate scooped her up into a tight hug, leaning her back into a dramatic kiss. She felt bad about having no dinner ready for him, not that it was the forties, but he set a paper bag down on the table in the entry way as he walked in, containing what she assumed was dinner.

"Sorry I didn't cook anything," she said. "I guess I'll have to learn how to cook something more than toast." She smiled sheepishly, and he planted another kiss on her lips.

"I proposed to you, knowing you couldn't cook. Don't think you have to change now. I mean, I wouldn't complain if you learned how to cook more dishes, but maybe it's something we can tackle together."

His smile completely melted her heart, and she was powerless to stop her arms from wrapping around his neck. She did not know what it was about him that was so irresistible, but she intended to spend her life finding out. Forgetting all about her and Candy's impossible plans for the following day, she let Tate lift her off of the ground, until her legs were around his waist, and carry her into the bedroom.

***

Coming out of their bedroom later that evening, breathless, Hazel found Candy plopped on the sofa with murder mysteries on the television. It was Candy's default setting. Candy arched an eyebrow dramatically when they shuffled out of the bedroom, hair disheveled and with less clothing than when they'd entered it.

"What?" Hazel asked, with a smirk she could not fight back. She felt giddy more often than she ever had before she and Tate got into a romantic relationship.

Tate walked up behind her and snuck a kiss to her cheek, a gesture that only made Candy's smile widen, before he left for the kitchen.

"What have you two been up to?" Candy asked in an obviously mischievous tone. Hazel blushed hard, covering her face with her hands. She started giggling, but tried to plan the perfect response.

Hazel straightened out her face as best as she could. "I climbed him like a tree," she said, before bursting out into laughter and falling onto the sofa. She and Candy laughed hysterically, causing Tate to run out of the kitchen trying to decipher the commotion.

"What's going on out here?" he asked, approaching the sofa with two plates of pasta. Both women stifled their remaining laughter, although Tate could only see Hazel. Candy vanished and then manifested her form on the chair across the room before Tate had a chance to sit directly on top of her. Not that she would have minded. She did always tease Hazel that she would manifest accidentally on top of him.

Over dinner, Hazel filled Tate in on her and Candy's plans for the next day. He was just glad she was not planning coffee with a serial killer, which was not out of the ordinary for her. She slept rather peacefully that night, with no spirit memories or nightmares invading her mind. Not knowing if it was just because the spirits had not found her yet, she was still grateful for the rest.

5

Friends from the Past

Getting ready for her meeting with Hera the next day, Hazel felt her stomach swirling. She may have even been more nervous than when she went to Harmony's salon, the woman who actually murdered Candy. It was never necessary for her to convince Harmony that Candy remained on earth as a spirit after she died, although Candy proved it when she used spectral powers to throw Harmony's gun after she shot Tate. She and Candy climbed into her car and headed into the city, unsure what to expect, but hoping for the best.

Hazel purposely chose a different coffee shop than the one where she met with Harmony, not that New Orleans was short in cafes. They chose to meet at a Café du Monde slightly outside of the city, which allowed her to avoid the bulk of the downtown traffic. She recognized Hera right away. Most customers did not sport pastel purple hair, even in the Big Easy. Although she held a position as a domestic violence social worker, Hera looked like someone who would have been friends with Candy. Both of them had brightly colored hair, and both of them were drop-dead gorgeous. Hazel felt admittedly self-conscious around such bombshells, although Candy was invisible to everyone but her. She approached Hera shyly, introducing herself and sitting at a table near the corner of the room.

Hera sat down hesitantly, reaching out to shake Hazel's hand.

"Hazel Watson?" she asked. "I'm Hera."

Hazel nodded her head, smiling. "I am. Thanks for meeting me."

"Anything for Candy."

Hazel looked over at Candy, who flashed her a tearful smile. She did not know what to say next, but it was not time for her introverted nature to paralyze her nerve.

"About that," Hazel started, "there's more to the reason I came here than what I said on messenger."

Hera eyed her warily. "Okay."

"I know what I'm about to say sounds... odd... but I need for you to trust me."

Hera maintained her silence, allowing Hazel to continue.

"I am an attorney... that was true, but I know Candy personally."

Hera's eyes softened. She leaned her elbows on the table.

"Really?"

Hazel hesitated. She hadn't expected Hera to play along with the conversation she had in her head. The anticipation Candy felt played into Hazel's own emotions. She felt them well up inside of her.

"So... sorry, this is hard to talk about." Hazel swallowed thickly. "I moved into Candy's old apartment a year ago. I didn't know her before she died."

Hera's eyes widened. Hazel continued. "There's something about me you don't know. Candy was still there..."

"What do you mean?" Hera's question held anticipation in it, like she already knew the answer. Hazel's heart was pounding within her ears, making it difficult to formulate her thoughts.

"Her spirit. She was still in the apartment. I can see her... I can see all of them, actually. I've always been able to."

Hazel's eyes fell to her hands. She expected Hera to run out of the café, but she did not. Instead, Candy's old friend sat quietly across the table, quietly pondering Hazel's claims. Surely, she saw the seriousness in Hazel's face. It was not as though Hazel looked like someone who would make such serious things up at someone else's expense.

"So," she paused. "What you're telling me is

that Candy's spirit was still in her apartment when you moved in?"

"Yes."

Hera nodded, keeping her eyes on Hazel. Hazel did her best to keep her composure, but her eyes betrayed her, allowing a single tear to escape the barrier she had built up. She dared to interrupt Hera's thoughts. She could not let her leave without believing her.

"Look... I know it's hard to believe. I've dealt with this all of my life." Hazel stopped to wipe tears that had begun falling from her eyes. "But I'm here today because Candy is one of the most important people in my life. She's my best friend, and she asked me to come today. We just moved out of her apartment, which I think has been hard for her, and she asked me to meet with you so she could get the stuff out of her storage unit. I had no idea she even had a storage container, but she said it was important to her."

Hazel's words gave Hera pause. She turned to scan the room before narrowing her eyes back in on Hazel.

"You know about her storage unit? How?" Hera's voice trailed off. Her eyes appeared to focus on nothing, as though she were looking into the past.

"She told me about it. I'm not making any of this up. She's here now."

Hera's eyes darted back to meet Hazel's. Hazel shot Candy a begging glance and Candy nodded before closing the distance to Hera and touching Hera's cheek. Hera shivered at Candy's touch, and her eyes widened even larger than they had been before. Hazel thought she could see fear, not fear of harm, but a deep realization that death was not the end. Hazel remained quiet, allowing Hera to collect her thoughts. She watched as her companion's eyes welled up with tears as Candy stroked her cheek.

"Did Candy tell you what we were doing on the night she died?"

Hera's voice had caught Hazel by surprise, but Candy quickly answered the question so Hazel could respond.

"Candy said the two of you worked at the bar the night she died, but she also said the two of you went out to Lavender Line the night before. Y'all brought Jake, and you tried to get him drunk." Hazel could not help but to laugh. "I'm sorry. It just sounds so much like something Candy would do."

Hera laughed as well, nodding her head. "Yeah. That was a fun night."

Hera wiped angrily at her tears.

"You know," Hazel began, "when Candy first met my fiancé... before he and I were a thing... Candy told me to tell him she would have climbed him like a tree if she were still alive."

Hera laughed heartily, still wiping at her tears. "Sounds about right. I could see her saying that. Damn, I miss her."

Hazel looked at Candy, who was wiping her own spectral tears.

"She's still here. I know you can't see her, but she can hear you."

Hera looked around, which reminded Hazel of how Tate always looked for Candy, but she turned up empty, just as he always did.

"It was so sad what happened to Jake. She really loved that guy, too," Hera said. "I'd imagine you heard what happened to him."

Hazel nodded. "Yes, it was really sad. I'm just glad we put the woman who killed them behind bars. Candy has been reunited with Jake, by the way. He came to her right after he died. They've been back together ever since."

Hera's eyes returned to their previous look of shock. "They're really together? That's amazing... I guess it's the best thing that could have happened out of a tragic situation."

Hazel smiled at Candy before returning her glance to Hera. "Yeah. It is. It was really hard on Candy... what happened to Jake, I mean. But they love each other still, and they've been building their relationship in this other stage of their existence. I wish you could see them together. He's been so good for her... she flirts with my fiancé a bit less now." Hazel smirked as Candy stuck out her tongue.

"I wish I could see her, too. Oh!" Hera's tone shifted to something more excited. "Tell her I'm engaged!"

"She knows!" Hazel tried to match Hera's excitement. "We saw the two of you on Facebook. She's quite nosy, so she was over my shoulder the entire time I was searching for you." Hazel laughed as Candy smacked at her for referring to her as nosy. "She was also gushing at how pretty you look and was glad you kept your purple hair."

Hera blushed before smiling wistfully. "She's beautiful too. She always was, inside and out. I would always tease her to cut that long hair. I can't imagine having hair to damn near my knees, but she seemed to love it. And the red... it was like fire. Perfect for Candy."

Hazel's heart fractured at the longing in Hera's voice. Hera glanced at her watch. "Oh," she hesitated, "I have a meeting in an hour, but I need to take you to Candy's storage unit... is that right?"

Hazel had forgotten all about the storage unit. "That would be great! We just moved into my fiancé's house, so Candy has own bedroom now. She wanted some of her things to make it more like home for her. I'm not sure what she wants out of it, though. I'm hoping, whatever it is, I can fit it in my car."

She looked up at Candy, who only shrugged her shoulders.

"Well, that's okay if you can't. You can always get anything else she needs later." Hera handed Hazel a business card. "And my cell is on here.

Please keep in contact with me, if you don't mind. I miss my friend and I would be so grateful if I could catch up with her... and with you... more."

Hazel grabbed the card and placed it in her satchel before reaching out to grab Hera's hand. Hera looked up to catch her eye. Her eyes looked mournful.

"I don't take this gift for granted, Hera. I'm so happy I could reunite you and Candy, even if it isn't in a way where you can see her. I have no problem keeping in contact with you, so the two of you can talk more. Shit... I need more friends. Maybe we can get together at my fiancé's house and have a triple date. If you think your fiancé would be open to the idea of Candy and Jake still being around. I know some people don't understand what I can do. I've had enough people treat me like I'm a crazy person to know that."

Hera shook her head vehemently. "Absolutely not. Adele is more into this stuff than I am! She goes on ghost tours and everything. I'll talk to her beforehand, though. Just to be make sure it's not awkward. Well, are you ready to follow me to the storage unit?"

Hera stood up from the table and pushed her chair back in as Hazel did the same.

6

Surprises in Storage

The drive to the storage container was only a few miles, although it took longer than expected in New Orleans traffic. Hazel watched the clock nervously, realizing Hera had an upcoming appointment and not wanting to make her late. Parking next to Hera's black sedan, Hazel jumped out of her car quickly, following Hera and Candy to the correct unit. Candy did not wait for the key to be turned to enter the metal room. Solid surfaces proved to be no barrier for her.

"Everything I removed out of her apartment is in here," Hera said as she opened the door. "I'd hoped her family would come for it, but I never heard from them. I left messages, and even sent letters, but I guess they did not want it."

The explanation made Hazel's heart ache. She had a strained relationship with her own family, but she could not imagine them leaving her belongings in storage if something happened to her. The thought reminded her she should probably tell her family about her engagement, but that was a problem for a later time.

"That's terrible. I can't imagine." She glanced at Candy, who was poking around in boxes, unphased by the conversation. "Candy told me about her family not going for her stuff. I know it upset her."

Hera nodded solemnly. "Yeah. I don't get it. Candy was an amazing person. Maybe it was too painful for her family to acknowledge. To be honest, we were best friends for years and I met none of them." Hera handed her a small silver key. "I wish I could stay, but I have to get to an appointment I can't miss. Can you please text me when you lock up? And please let me know when you'd like to get together again. If Candy can hear me... I love you, Candy."

Hazel hesitantly took the key, surprised it was being offered to her. She was sure she would blow the plan they had haphazardly made, but hadn't.

"I absolutely will. I'll text you when I lock up, but please let me know when you are free and would like to get together. I've taken time off of work so I'm probably available more often than you are." She smiled at Hera as Hera nodded and exited the storage room.

After watching Hera walk away, Hazel approached Candy, who was headfirst into a stack of boxes.

"What are you looking for?" she asked, opening the box Candy was submerged in.

"I'm looking for my photos."

"Oh, well, let me help you."

Pulling a stool next to the box, Hazel dug into the box with Candy overlooking her search.

"It's in a smaller box with flowers on it. There

isn't that much stuff in here, so I'm guessing it's in one of these boxes."

"We'll find them. So, what did you think about seeing Hera again?"

Candy laid her head on Hazel's shoulder and Hazel planted a kiss on her forehead.

"I thought it would hurt more than it did. It was exciting to see her again, but I wish she could see me, or hear me."

"She felt you, though. When you touched her on the face."

Hazel felt Candy nod her head gently. "Yeah. That was something."

"It was probably what tipped the scales, honestly. I was worried she would run out of the restaurant." Hazel flipped a stack of papers over inside the box and saw a hint of a floral pattern beneath. She smiled as she reached both hands inside and pulled out a flower print box.

"You found it!" Candy's head lifted as she shot forward to get a better look. "Thank you!"

Hazel carried the box over to a small table across the room and opened it. Pictures of her beautiful red-headed friend filled the box, making it impossible for Hazel to fight back tears.

She had seen very few pictures of when Candy was alive, and although they were beautiful, they broke her heart.

"Oh, wow." Candy hovered just over her shoulder. "Can you help me hang some of these in my room? There are pictures of me with Hera and Jake. I'd like those to be up where I can see them. Jake is gonna love these!"

"Absolutely," Hazel replied as she thumbed through some of the photos. Candy tried to manipulate the photos, but got frustrated with her inability to move things like she wanted to, so she pulled her hand away.

"Can you dig to the bottom of the box and see if there's anything down there, specifically an envelope?"

"Sure."

Hazel dug through the box, flipping what seemed like hundreds of pictures onto their sides until she reached the bottom, where a brown envelope was lying flat underneath the contents. When she went to grab the envelope, which appeared to have some weight to it, she pulled her hand back. Instead, she pointed at it. "You're in luck. It's still where you left it."

Candy smiled, leaning over to touch the envelope. "Outstanding! Open it." She gestured to Hazel to open the envelope, but Hazel was hesitant. She did not know what it was about the object that gave her pause. "Open it!"

Candy's voice held excitement, but Hazel suddenly felt anxious. She reached a shaking hand into the box and grabbed the envelope, pulling it out of the box slowly. It had more weight to it than she expected.

"This may have sat in here forever, but I want you to have it. There's no way for me to use it for its original purpose anymore."

Hazel tilted her head to the side, still holding the unopened envelope, feeling the curiosity grow within her.

"You're giving whatever is in this envelope to me?"

"Yes! Open it already!"

Candy had started bouncing up and down, unable to control the excitement Hazel did not understand.

Opening the envelope gently, Hazel tried to refrain from tearing it while Candy leaned over her with a chin resting on her shoulder.

Peeling the flap closure of the envelope open, Hazel gasped. Hundred-dollar bills were stacked neatly within the unassuming envelope. How many? She did not know. She stared, open-mouthed, at the money resting within her hand.

"Candy..." Hazel trailed off as her mouth opened and closed like a fish out of water. "What is this?"

Candy let out a sound that was a mixture of a giggle and a throat clearing. "My college fund." She glared into Hazel's eyes before smirking. "Oh, my goodness, Hazel. I wasn't a drug dealer or something! My family wanted me to go to college, so they released my trust, but I never had the chance to go. I wasn't ready yet... I was too busy enjoying my life. Now it's yours."

Hazel still stared at the stack of bills in her hand as though she were watching something she was not supposed to see but could not turn away from. "Candy... I can't take this."

Candy scoffed. "You can, and you will. My parents don't need it, and it's mine. They gave it to me. Consider it an investment in your victim helping business. You're going to need money to leave your career. I know Tate intended to take care of you by himself, but this way you can contribute. I can contribute."

Hazel was speechless. She had yet to remove the money from the envelope surrounding it.

"How much money is this? This is too much, Candy."

Candy bent over until her line of sight was parallel to the money in Hazel's hand. She smiled mischievously. "I think this envelope contains close to ten thousand dollars, but..."

Before Candy finished her statement, Hazel dropped the stack of money, causing it to fall out of the envelope and scatter onto the floor. Her heart beat viciously in her throat. She fell to her knees and haphazardly tried to scoop it back up. Candy watched her with amusement.

"But there should be more envelopes scattered throughout this unit with more money."

Candy sounded pleased with herself, but Hazel's heart was racing as she clumsily piled the bills back into the partially torn envelope. She thought she might throw up.

"Didn't you use banks?" Hazel's voice came out more hysterical than she intended.

"No way, doll. At least not for most of my

money. I never trusted my family not to find a way to bleed me dry if I pissed them off, which I gladly did every chance I got."

Hazel returned to her legs, although they were shaky.

"Damn, Candy. Your family sounds more messed up than mine."

Candy shot her a sideways glance. "You have no idea. Us black sheep have to stick together, right?" Candy nudged Hazel with her shoulder, causing Hazel to shiver. "Hey... snap out of it, Hazel. This is a good thing. You can leave your miserable job and focus your attention solely on what you were born to do. I would not want anyone else to have this money."

***

After finding what Candy believed to be all of her hidden envelopes, they had uncovered close to forty thousand dollars. Hazel's shock loomed over her like a cloud during the entire drive home. Other than the money, photos, and a few personal items, Candy left the rest of her belongings in the unit for another day. Hazel sent a text message to Hera, as she had promised to do, not only letting her know they were leaving, but also offering to take over the contract for the unit. Although she knew the money was Candy's, she did not enjoy feeling as though she had taken money from Hera.

She could not believe that money had been sitting secretly in that unit for over a year. The entire situation was unbelievable. At first, she thought about keeping the money's existence a secret, but it did not take long for her to decide to tell Tate. She did not want there to be secrets in their relationship, especially not with them getting married. Before she began planning the conversation in her head, her cell phone rang, pulling her back into the present.

"Hazel, I need to talk to you." Tate's voice sounded panicked on the phone. Hazel's face faltered as she dropped into a chair. He was calling her from work, which was unusual. Usually, he sent her text messages when at work.

"What's going on?" Her nervousness was reflected in her voice.

Tate cleared his throat, and then lowered his voice so she had to strain to hear him. "Another woman went missing."

Her heart dropped with his admission as her hand instinctively flew up to cup her mouth.

"Oh, no! Do they think the same person who took her also killed the other two women?"

"Yes. Her name is Michelle Barrilleaux. She was at a fishing camp with her family in the Honey Island area. She went out to take a walk with her dog and never returned."

Hazel felt sick to her stomach. She hesitated.

"We have to find her before he kills her. I don't know how, but we have to."

"I know. Do you think you can get more information from Emily or Malerie? I know they didn't see his face, but what about more information about where they were kept?"

"I can try. They were both blindfolded, so I don't think they can tell us much about where they were kept. They could see the inside of the building, but not the outside."

Tate let out an audible breath. "Okay. Well, I love you and I'll see you when I get home."

"I love you too."

As Hazel hung up the phone, she felt defeated. Her gift, as some would call it, had allowed her to help many spirits, but it often only created a situation in which she was always haunted, but helpless. She could only see what the spirits could see, and sometimes that was not much, but she wished she could do more. Malerie warned her, but she was powerless to stop the new abduction. Her thoughts of telling Tate about the money went to the back of her mind after Tate's phone call, hidden behind the shadow of another victim.

7

Possibilities and Pressure

Hazel spent the rest of the time while Tate was at work unpacking her boxes and finding a place for her belongings. She and Candy stored the money in Candy's bedroom for the time being, at least until she spoke to Tate about it. At least until she decided what to do with it. The possibilities were endless, but she and Candy both agreed they should invest the money into something that would make money for her and help her help others. It was the best option if it was going to help her stay out of the Public Defender's Office, a career she wanted to give up for good. She did not know what that would look like, but hoped Tate could help her with that decision.

Putting a frozen casserole in the oven, Hazel and Candy sat down on the sofa and flipped on the evening news. Tate would be home any minute and she was tired of unpacking. She expected them to break the news about an abduction, so she wanted to get more information about the missing woman. As she expected, the abduction of Michelle Barrilleaux was one of the first stories featured.

The woman was beautiful, just like Malerie and Emily. Her deep brown eyes were a striking contrast to her light hair. Unlike the first two victims, Michelle was said to have disappeared from her family's fishing camp on Pearl River. Pearl river was near Honey Island swamp, so Hazel wondered if the killer changed his hunting location after the discovery of Malerie and Emily's bodies. The police made the same assumption, connecting the first two murders to her disappearance quickly.

They gave information about the missing woman, as well as a tip line for anyone who had information on the three cases. They also announced a planned search for the missing woman the next day. Even though the thought terrified her, Hazel decided without question to join the search. She hoped Tate would join her, since he did not have to work the next day. His company would make her feel safer.

When Tate got home, she rushed to the door to greet him. The world could be so cruel and unpredictable, which made her appreciate him so much more. Tate was kind. She could always count on him. In such a world, that was everything.

The casserole was good, but it reminded her she needed to learn how to cook food from scratch. Thankfully, Tate appreciated the dinner regardless. After dinner, they moved to the living room to watch a little television before bed. Her heart raced at the thought of bringing up the money and at the thought of the search the next morning. She wanted to help in any way she could, but the thought of being back in the Louisiana wetlands freaked her out. Stemming from her own abduction in the swamp, it was not something she ever thought she would get over.

She reached over to mute the television. Turning to look at Tate, she bit back her hesitation.

"Hey... I needed to talk to you about something... well, a few things."

His eyebrow arched curiously. "Okay... what's up?"

"I saw the news broadcast about Michelle Barrilleaux."

Tate nodded somberly, setting his hand on her leg but remaining silent to let her talk.

"They announced a search for her tomorrow... I wondered if you were up for it."

"If you want to do it, then I am for it." He squeezed her leg gently, looking deeply into her eyes. "I'm proud of you for wanting to do that. It's really brave of you after everything you've been through."

She hugged him, grateful for his closeness and constant support. "Thank you, Tate. I don't know what I'd do without you."

He kissed her on her cheek, lingering near her face for a while and whispering in her ear. "I'll always be there for you. You know that."

The thought of the stack of cash in Candy's bedroom returned to her mind, making her uneasy. She shifted in her seat.

"There's something else I needed to tell you, but I think I'd rather show you."

His head tilted curiously as his hand lingered on her. "Okay... now you've got me curious."

Standing up from the sofa, she reached out a hand and escorted him to Candy's bedroom door. Knocking to get Candy's permission to walk in, she brought Tate to the closet door, and pulled out the floral box that was on the shelf. Candy perked up on the bed when she saw what was happening. She, too, was curious about how Tate would react.

"I told you I was going to meet with Candy's friend Hera today... right?"

"Yeah. I forgot to ask you about how that went, although it appears you brought something back, so I'm assuming she didn't run the other way." His eyes were expectant as he eyed the box in her hand.

"You could say that," she said, biting her lip nervously. "She didn't run. Actually, with Candy's help, she believed me. We talked for a while. She was really nice and excited about reconnecting with Candy. We ended up going to Candy's storage unit before Hera left for a meeting. She left Candy and I there so we could look around. Candy led me to this." Hazel opened the box and watched as the size of Tate's eyes doubled. He sputtered, clearly as speechless as she had been when she first saw the box's contents.

He reached out to touch the bills, opening and closing his mouth a few times but not finding the words to say.

"Candy said this money was from her trust fund for college, but she never had the chance to go, or waited, in any case. She said she wanted me to have it, since she had no more use for it. She wants me to use it while I'm out of work... to help others like her."

She quieted and waited for Tate's response. He scanned the room instinctively, looking for his invisible roommate, but he did not see her and returned his gaze to Hazel.

"Wow." His voice was incredulous. "Is she here?"

Hazel nodded and indicated towards the bed.

He looked back towards the bed and smiled. "Thank you, Candy. I wish we could do more for you, after everything you've done for Hazel."

He returned his eyes to Hazel, who was sitting silently beside him on the floor. "I know you will put this to good use, and you'll help many people without the strain of your career. I support whatever you and Candy choose to do with it."

"Damn straight," said Candy from the bed.

Hazel looked up at her and smiled brightly, telling Tate what Candy said. He nodded and pulled her into a hug. Candy hopped off the bed and joined in, Tate shivering at her touch.

"That was just Candy... she did always tell me she would land on top of you."

Tate chuckled, but Candy swatted Hazel on the arm.

Setting the lid back on the box, Tate stood back up.

"Maybe we should put this in the safe in my office. Would you be okay with that?"

Hazel glanced at Candy, who nodded her head. "Yes. That's a good idea."

Both women followed Tate to his office where he showed them how to open the safe, in case they ever needed to take money out of it. She tried to commit the combination and opening method to memory, having not used a lock like that since she was in high school.

"So, are you ready for bed?" Tate asked, stifling a yawn.

"I'll meet you in there. I just want to talk to Candy about tomorrow." She gave Tate a kiss before he told Candy goodnight and walked away.

"What's going on tomorrow, doll?" Candy asked, as she led their way back to her bedroom. She looked up at Hazel anxiously as she plopped back onto her bed.

Hazel explained what was going on with the new missing woman and what her and Tate's intentions were in joining the search. Candy offered to not only join in the search, but also to invite Jake to tag along. Knowing Candy and Tate would be there with her made Hazel feel a little better about venturing into a place she had only ever seen in her nightmares, sleeping and awake.

***

Digging into the cool dirt, she felt excited about having a colorful flowerbed again. The deep freezes over the winter had killed all but her roses. It was amazing how frigid winters could get in the deep south of Louisiana, even though most summer days felt like a sauna. Wiping the sweat from her brow with a rag, she scanned the bank of the swamp, narrowing her gaze on a great blue heron. Movement in the trees caught her attention, causing the enormous bird to drop its fish and fly away.

A large form, covered in thick hair and swamp weeds, trudged through the moss-covered trees. Her pulse raced as she crouched behind the rose bushes and watched it quietly. She was too scared to breathe, too scared it would hear her racing heart. It was only about a hundred yards away from her, but was across the narrow canal. She wondered if it would chase her if she ran. Building up her courage to flee, she rose to her feet and ran into her back door, bolting the latch behind her and praying it wouldn't follow.

8

The Date
and the
Ghost

Pulling on their rain boots, Hazel and Tate
waited for directions for the search party to look
for the missing woman, Michelle Barrilleaux.
The authorities did not have any evidence she
was dead, nor had Hazel seen her spirit, but they
had to start somewhere. Michelle had been
missing for a few days, under the same
circumstances as Malerie and Emily, so the

police believed they would only find her body. It was Hazel's first time joining an official search effort, but she did not know how else to help. A knot had been twisting in her stomach since she opened her eyes that morning.

Still reeling from her nightmare the previous night, she was even more hesitant to venture into the swamp than she had been when she had first decided to join. The dream had at least given her a glimpse at the figure Emily referred to as a swamp monster, but Hazel was not any closer to knowing if it had only been a really tall man in a suit. Real or not, she could feel Emily's fear while watching the beast, and Emily believed it to be exactly what she called it. She hadn't even mentioned the last nightmare to Tate because she wanted to at least pretend to be in better control of her mind than she was.

There were dozens of people there from Pearl River and the surrounding areas. There were people on foot, as well as in off-road vehicles, pirogues, and motorboats. Candy and Jake tagged along, hoping they could help. They did not have the same restrictions as living people did and could get to places difficult to traverse.

One man stood out among the group, Emily's husband, Joshua. He stood away from the crowd with his face set in what looked like determination. His presence filled Hazel with dread. His wife's body had only just been found, but Hazel could understand why he was there. If Michelle was found, then maybe Emily's killer would be caught. She had only ever seen him in memory transfer dreams, but she knew it was him.

The swamp brought back a flurry of terrible memories for Hazel, but she tried to swallow her reservations back for the good of the missing woman. She knew what it was like to be a missing woman. That realization caused terror to snake around her, filling her with a sickening feeling, making it hard to breathe.

It had only been a few months since Hazel had been a victim of abduction, and was held captive in the swamp, just as her abductor's previous four victims. He had killed those other women and buried them in the same swamp where Hazel waited for her own death. If it hadn't been for the spirit of those victims, and the spectral energy they used to attack Raymond Waters and delay his attack, she probably would not be alive. It was a fact she couldn't forget.

Intertwining his fingers in hers, Tate realized her hesitation and pulled her into a hug.

"We don't have to do this, love," he said, a look of concern flooding his face. "This can't be easy for you."

Hazel nodded and allowed herself to be surrounded by one of his bear hugs.

"I'm okay. I need to do this."

He planted a kiss on her lips and then gently squeezed her hand before turning to face the forward marching line of searchers.

"If you change your mind, just say the word. I'll get you out of here if you need to leave."

"Okay. Thank you, Tate. Thank you for everything. I love you."

He smiled, passing a hand on her cheek. She felt chills race down her body.

"I love you too."

They wandered around the marsh for hours, but there were no signs of the missing woman. Hazel wondered if Michelle could still be alive, or if the killer decided to dump her body somewhere else since his other two victims had been discovered so close to where she had been abducted. Either possibility was equally likely. Climbing into Tate's car after the search, and preparing for the near hour drive home, all Hazel could do was hope that Michelle's spirit would not appear to her once she closed her eyes.

As they got into the city, Tate took an unexpected turn off the freeway.

"Where are we going?" she asked, genuinely unsure of the answer.

He smiled, reaching over to take her hand.

"It's been a rough couple of days, but I thought we deserved a little celebration. I packed us an overnight bag in the trunk. I reserved a room at the Omni hotel downtown. We can do whatever you want, but I thought we could maybe check out the art museum and grab some dinner. I hope that's okay. We could go home if you're too tired and do it another night. It's up to you."

The butterflies returned to her stomach as she shook her head vigorously. "We will absolutely not go home after you went through all of that trouble. I'm tired, but that's nothing a shower and coffee can't fix."

He squeezed her hand gently. His smile had gotten brighter. "Well, alright. It's a date."

His response made Hazel giggle. He had asked her on dates for the first several years of their friendship, but she had always taken it as a joke. She never really believed he would want a relationship with her. It was something that still shocked her. She was glad they waited to get romantically involved, however. They were now both nearly thirty years old, and she hoped the maturity they had developed over the past several years would aid in the success of their future together.

Hazel was blown away at the sight of the immense historic hotel as they pulled up to leave Tate's car with the valet. She did not know the age of the hotel, but she knew it was from another time. The horse and buggy out front made her feel like a time traveler. She could not remember ever staying anywhere so fancy. Tate pulled a small suitcase out of the trunk, and she snickered.

"I had zero idea you had snuck that in there."

"Magic," he said as he flourished it in front of her before reaching for her hand. "Shall we?"

Looking down at the mud on her clothes, she did not even know if she was clean enough to walk into the lobby of the hotel, but they trudged in any way.

Her jaw dropped when she saw the opulence of the inside of the building. There were two grand staircases along the side wall with a giant crystal chandelier hanging just above them. Intricately carved statues stood sentinel everywhere she looked. She turned in circles, taking it all in, while Tate checked in at the reception desk. A large water feature adorned the entrance, and the sound of the falling water filled the vast space. She felt a bit out of place in such a beautiful space, but she bit back her self-doubt.

Tate slid an arm around her waist as she stared at one of the large statues. "Ready?" he asked as he began guiding her to the stairs.

"I think I may be too dirty to walk around this place."

"Well, let's get you clean, then. I think I grabbed everything you need."

She nodded as they headed towards the staircases and ascended to their room. Their room was on the second floor, so it was not a far walk. The king-sized bed took up nearly the entire room, but the view of the downtown area out of the window was breathtaking. Opening the glass door, she walked out onto the small balcony and took in the view of the city below. Up close, some parts of New Orleans could be dreadful, but from her current vantage point, she could see why millions of people flocked to The Big Easy every year.

"This would be a beautiful place to have coffee in the morning," she said, smiling as much on the inside as she was on the outside. The thoughts of the three victims still sat on her subconscious mind, but the unexpected getaway forced them to a dark corner. At least for the time being.

"We will definitely have to take our coffee out here in the morning, and the good news is that it's not supposed to be raining."

"Well, isn't that a pleasant surprise?" She smirked as he stood behind her and wrapped his arms around her.

"I have a confession to make," he said, resting his chin on her head. She turned to look at him curiously.

"Oh, really? Let's have it then."

He pulled her back close, planting a kiss on her lips.

"I've had this reservation for a few weeks." He smiled bashfully, causing her to blush. "I planned on proposing to you here."

She felt her insides melt into a big vat of pudding as she squeezed him and never wanted to let go. "Oh, really? Well... I'm pretty partial to the way you ended up doing it. I think I may have needed rescuing that day, but I appreciate this day no less."

He wrapped his arm around her shoulders and led her back inside. "Shower or bath? I reckon we should be clean before our stench infiltrates this fancy ass room."

"Your stench!" she teased as she playfully smacked him on the butt and ran into the bathroom.

***

Leaving the bathroom with five pounds less grime on her, Hazel towel dried her hair as she dug through the suitcase Tate packed secretly for their overnight romantic getaway. She was surprised to see he left no stone unturned, bringing multiple outfits for her to choose from. Candy would have frowned at the fashion choices, but they were Hazel's favorites. Candy would have chosen sexier outfits than Hazel owned, but Tate packed her jeans and comfortable tops and one dress, just in case she was up to it. He knew her so well. Her hair dryer and small makeup bag, which contained only the essentials, were tucked into the small compartment in the outer cover of the case. He had allowed her to shower first, so she dried her hair and attempted to get herself semi-beautified before he got out of the bathroom.

Having never been to the art museum since she moved to New Orleans, she was excited to visit it. It was getting late in the afternoon, however, so she did not know how much time they would have before it closed. Also, knowing there was a statue garden outside of the museum, so she was excited to see it as well. She had been in New Orleans since she was in undergraduate school, but she had admittedly never seen many of the touristy sights, being too introverted for that. But her relationship with Tate brought her out of her shell, at least when she was with him, so she was open to more adventures. Preferably non-dangerous ones.

After Tate got out of the shower, they set off for their date. The museum was in City Park, which made her think back to when Tate met her there one night, when she had only just started looking into the disappearance of Angela Spencer. Angela was the murder victim who was haunting her then client, Roy Miller. Angela's killer had thrown Hazel's life into chaos, but she tried to not focus on that fact. Instead, she thought about meeting with Tate that night and how it made her feel, how much she wanted to be with him, yet how scared she was to tell him. She now knew he felt the same way about her, but she never imagined it then. Even Candy seemed to see it, but neither she nor Tate realized they were meant to be together. When she looked at them now, it seemed like ancient history.

Like the hotel, the museum was expansive and historic. The columns lining the entrance and the large fountain surrounded by the circle driveway transported her to Ancient Rome. The Roman theme followed into the interior of the museum, which was immense, like the room that would have housed a Roman bath during the time of the Caesars.

A balcony wrapped the entire inside of the Great Hall, which was what the museum called their large entrance area. Grand staircases led visitors to the upper level and rooms broke off from the main entrance in every direction. She did not know which way to go first, so she allowed Tate to take the lead, trusting he knew his way around.

By the time the museum was about to close, she was not sure if they had seen everything it offered, but they had certainly wandered around aimlessly, saw priceless art and artifacts from across time and place, and had even grabbed coffee at the little café tucked away in one of the museum's corners. The sun was setting by the time they walked out the front doors, but they still made their way around the side of the building to look at the sculpture garden.

Heading back to the car once it got too dark, they went to an eclectic pasta restaurant Hazel had been to once before. She liked the place because it was not too fancy or busy, so she and

Tate could enjoy their meal without the stress of being around many people, or without her feeling underdressed.

On the way back to the hotel, Hazel could not help but to periodically glance into the back seat. Maybe she was expecting to see Candy sitting there, although she and Jake had left before they drove away from the search, or maybe her anxiety about the darkened space behind her drew her eyes to check for silent passengers. She did not know which.

Candy would not disrupt their date, and was probably back at the house with Jake, but it was instinctual for Hazel to look for her. Each time she flicked her eyes up to look into the mirror, the back seat was empty, until it was not.

She screamed as a pair of green eyes met her glance from the seat behind her. Slamming on the breaks, Tate just barely missed a rear end collision as he eased the car onto the shoulder. The face was gone, but Hazel's entire body shook as her breath came in short bursts. Tate reached out to her, caressing her hair gently with his hands. She could not hide the terror in her eyes and frantically looked into the backseat repeatedly, expecting to see the woman there again.

"What's wrong?" His voice remained calm as he caressed her head to calm her. He followed her eyes to the backseat, but could not see what she saw.

She could not respond as tears poured from her eyes. Cars zipped by them on the street, increasing her anxiety. The last thing they needed was to get side swiped.

"Sweetie, what's wrong?" He hugged her as she desperately tried to calm herself.

"There was a woman." She struggled to keep her voice even. "A woman in the backseat."

Tate looked confused, glancing into the backseat again. A taxi driver honked their horn as they passed too close to Tate's car. He and Hazel both flinched.

"Hold on, love. Let me get us somewhere safer. You're okay. It's going to be okay." She nodded as he waited for an opening in the traffic and then gingerly pulled the car back onto the street. He faced ahead, but his hand still gently grazed her hair. She closed her eyes and tried to focus on his calming touch.

"The hotel is only a few blocks away... would it be okay if I waited to pull over until we got there? This traffic is hectic."

She nodded, but kept her eyes closed as he rubbed her head, not wanting to see the woman again. She did not recognize the woman, but it was not Michelle Barrilleaux, who she had searched for in the swamp that morning. Having never seen the green-eyed woman in her life, she could not image where the woman had come from. Had she followed them from the museum? The restaurant? The swamp? The possibilities were endless, but they swirled in Hazel's head while Tate drove.

The second time pulling into the luxury hotel felt different from the first and Hazel was angry at the ghost for interrupting her date night with Tate. Could they enjoy one full day without a spirit barging into her life? The incident caused toxic thoughts to flood Hazel's brain, thoughts about the way spirits had affected her parents' marriage. Her parents were hanging on by codependency and nothing else, a fate she swore would never come to her and Tate. As Tate pulled the car up to the valet, she snapped out of her shame spiral, opening her eyes for the first time since leaving the shoulder of the street.

Walking around to her side of the car, he opened the door and pulled her into a hug before guiding her out of the way so the valet could move the car. Her tears had stopped falling and her breathing had stabilized, fully thanks to Tate's gentle caresses through her hair. Before she started dating Tate, it was Candy who always rubbed her hair when she was upset. It only made sense for Tate to pick up on the fact that it was the trick to calming her.

"We can go to the room. I'm okay," she said as Tate stopped outside of the building, unsure if she was ready to talk about what happened.

He nodded, kissed her cheek, then wrapped his arm back around her and walked her up the stairs and into their room. She dreaded even talking about it. The thought kept plaguing her that one more spirit would be too many for him, and he would run away. The other side of her fought that thought every time it clouded her mind. Tate loved her and had for a long time by his own admission. He knew what he was getting into with her, but he proposed to her, anyway.

He would not leave her because of her abilities. She knew that, but she still had to remind herself repeatedly or her own self-doubt would spiral her down like a feather on the wind.

Guiding her to the bed, Tate sat down and then gently pulled her down next to him. He did not force her to talk and, instead, just let her curl up against him. She reveled in the warmth of his body. Although her voice was still shaky, she broke the silence.

"I'm sorry I scared you."

He pulled her in closer, kissing her on the top of her head. "Don't apologize. I'm just sorry whatever happened... happened. Did you see a spirit in the car?"

She nodded, burying her head deeper into his chest. "I didn't expect to see anyone in the backseat, but I kept feeling the need to look. I didn't expect to see eyes staring back at me. It caught me by surprise, I guess."

"Did you recognize her? Was it Michelle?"

She shook her head, seeing the woman's face in her mind again. "That was the thing that scared me the most, I think. It wasn't Michelle. I didn't recognize her at all. I don't know who she was or where she came from. I don't know if she found me in the museum... the swamp... I just don't know how long she'd been following me before she showed up."

Tate's eyebrows furrowed, but he started petting her hair again.

"Did she say anything?"

"No. She was literally there and then she was gone."

"I'm sorry that happened to you. I would have screamed too. So, she's gone now?"

"Yes."

"Good. Are you starting to feel a bit better?"

She pulled away from him enough to look into his eyes before kissing him deeply. He moaned happily against her lips.

"She's gone, and I am already angry at her for interrupting our night. I'll think about her tomorrow, but I don't want to dedicate any more time to her tonight."

"Did I mention I love you?"

She smiled against his lips, suddenly finding it impossible to fight the pull of his body on her.

"I love you too."

***

Waking up the next morning, Hazel was surprised to have suffered no nightmares over the night, although she did not know why. She had fully expected one of the many spirits who haunted her to show her their memories while she was powerless to stop them. She hoped they were just being considerate, but she knew that was probably not the case. Spirits did not tend to care about inconveniencing her, at least not in her view. Rolling over, she noticed Tate already sitting on the outside balcony.

Grabbing a pajama from the chair, she walked outside to join him. He turned at the sound of the door and motioned for her to sit on his lap. She happily obliged, leaning into his embrace.

"Did you sleep okay? Any nightmares?"

"Surprisingly, no. I slept great."

***

After having a room service breakfast on the balcony, they headed back to their house on the outskirts of the city. Even with the terrifying experience on their way back from dinner the night before, Hazel felt refreshed from their romantic night on the town. An entire night without nightmares helped. She knew she had a goofy grin on her face during the ride home, but there was no spirit in the backseat, so she did not care. Candy would undoubtedly interrogate her for the dirty details of their date, and she thought she just might share.

9

Disruptions
and
Distractions

Tate and Hazel spent the rest of their Sunday at home with Candy and Jake, their own version of a double date. Tate did not seem to mind her interpreting any conversations between the living and the dead. He was a better sport than most people in such a strange situation. As they sat on the sofa that night watching the local news, breaking news flashed across the screen.

Tate raised the volume on the television, thinking it was an update on the missing woman, Michelle Barrilleaux, but it was not. Instead, they announced the discovery of the body of another woman.

"Tonight, the body of another woman was found in the Pearl River area. This is a picture of thirty-six-year-old mother of two, Jessica Barrios. The body was discovered by a group of fishermen early this morning. Mrs. Barrios was visiting her family's fishing camp in Pearl River when she went missing. Authorities are encouraging all who can leave the Pearl River area to do so until the suspect is caught. To those who cannot leave the area, practice extreme caution. Police suspect the same person responsible for the murders of Emily Landry and Malerie Ledet, as well as the disappearance of Michelle Barrilleaux, is also to blame for the death of Jessica Barrios. The body of Mrs. Michelle Barrilleaux has yet to be found. If you have any information to help police apprehend the person responsible for these heinous crimes, please contact the number at the bottom of your screen."

Tate lowered the volume on the television as Hazel stared at the screen, unable to turn away from the familiar green eyes in the photograph that was displayed across the television. Ten numbers were placed at the very bottom of her photo. It was the tip line for those who had information to help find her killer, but Hazel could not call it. Even if she had any clue who the killer was, or how to find Michelle, she still did not know how to help the authorities to find him unless they believed in her gifts.

"It's her," Hazel said, barely over her breath. Her words startled Tate. He looked at her with his eyes wide.

"The woman they just reported is her? Jessica Barrios, was it?"

Hazel nodded. "I think she followed us from the swamp. That's where she must have found me."

"But you still haven't seen Michelle Barrilleaux?"

She shook her head, but she felt dazed. "I need to be able to work with the police. I need them to believe in my abilities. If I could work with them, then maybe we could help these women and find their killer. Maybe we could find Michelle."

Tate pursed his lips, and she could tell he was thinking, but his finger drew sweet circles over her wrist. Sitting quietly, she let him gather his thoughts. He was a police officer, so if anyone knew how to get her acquainted with the police, it was him. After a few moments, he turned to look at her. His face set with determination.

"Let me talk to some people. Everyone doesn't have to believe in your abilities for you to be able to work with the department. We don't need everyone; we just need the right person. I may know who that person is. I'm going to talk to him."

Hazel's eyes lit up as she leaned closer to him.

"Who is it?"

"His name is Jeremiah Bourgeois. He's a detective. I think you may know his wife. She owns Bourgeois realty. I think she is the one who leased Candy's apartment to you."

Samantha Bourgeois had leased her apartment to her, after keeping the apartment off of the market for months because it was haunted. Plus, Candy would terrorize anyone who tried to view it. If her husband believed in spirits as much as she did, Hazel thought she may just have a shot at convincing him to work with her. She smiled as the excitement rose in her, excitement at the possibility of being able to help the murdered women in more ways than just letting them invade her head and personal space.

"That could work! His wife believes in spirits for sure! She wouldn't even rent the apartment out for months because Candy was terrorizing everyone who tried to view it." She laughed and Tate followed suit. "She was even too scared to go into the apartment when potential tenants were inside getting remote controls thrown at them! She stayed in the hall the entire time!"

Before they knew it, they had both fallen into giggles at Samantha Bourgeois' expense. Even Candy and Jake, who heard the commotion, came back into the living room to join in. They were all in stitches, laughing about how much Candy scared away people who entered her apartment when they were trying to rent it.

"One woman even pissed on herself!" Candy shrieked before rolling over in a rumble of laughter that had her rocking on the floor. Hazel barely repeated what she said for Tate before spitting her water all over the place. Candy had more stories than even Hazel had realized, and all she wished was that Tate would be able to see Candy tell these stories while rolling and kicking on the floor laughing. Just Candy's thrashing, laughing appearance was worthy of a viral video.

By the time they all stopped laughing, Candy and Jake had to flicker out of visibility due to low energy. Hazel and Tate were drenched with sweat and still trying to catch their breath. She had so much fun spending time laughing with Tate, Candy and Jake and she felt hopeful about helping the police. All she wanted to do was take her fiancé to bed and continue their romantic weekend in their own bedroom.

So, as Candy and Jake vanished to conserve their energy, Hazel straddled Tate's lap, and pulled him into a passionate kiss. The taste was divine and his pheromones that filled her senses made her crave more of him. Judging by the movement of his body, he felt the same way. Lifting her up, he walked with her legs wrapped around his waist, with her lips on his, all the way into their bedroom, kicking the door closed behind them.

They could barely wait to be alone together and started hungrily tearing off each other's clothes before they even made it to the bed. There was an almost animalistic need to be with each other, to be connected in a primal way. The ecstasy he gave her that night made electricity flow through her entire body, even into her face, and she had to rest her senses once it finally fizzled.

She did not care about him seeing her naked once the lights came on anymore. He loved her, and it was time for her to stop being shy around him. She was elated, content, and exhausted, so she went to bed with her bare body laid against his bare body, with most of the blankets hanging off the bed. Every trace of his fingertip, even up her arm, was electric, so she reveled in every single touch he graced her with. They laid in bed for hours that night, just touching each other gently and kissing each other, and basking in how it felt to have such powerful chemistry with someone. She fell asleep with her head on his chest, while he drew loving patterns on her back with the tips of his fingers.

10

Gift Unmasked

A slamming door startled her awake. She gasped, and her eyes searched the space for an intruder, but she did not see anyone. Her head felt fuzzy, as though she had been drugged. She did not recognize her surroundings, but did not feel the strength to lift her body off the mattress on the floor. Instead, she laid there, hoping whoever had slammed the door stayed away until she built up her strength.

She did a mental assessment of her body, trying to find injuries she may have, but the drugs almost gave *her the sensation of paralysis. Her limbs felt numb. She could see her arms and legs, and they were there, but they did not want to function as they should. She wiggled her fingers and toes, just to be sure, but it was all she could do. Her eyes shot around the room, scanning her prison from where she laid. It looked to be an old fishing shack, haphazardly built out of wood. There was only one room, with a bucket instead of a bathroom. The mattress on the floor, and a wooden chair, were the only furniture. She felt a numbness in her chest, a fact which she was glad for. She knew if her emotions broke through, they would debilitate her.*

***

Hazel was not expecting the face peering down at her when she jolted awake.

"Candy?" she muttered, rubbing her eyes vigorously before pulling the blankets over her naked body.

Candy flopped down on the bed next to her. "That's right, sunshine. Good thing Tate left for work because you were making quite a fuss in here. And where are your clothes?"

Hazel's brain was still fuzzy. Spirit memories did that to her.

"Sorry..."

"What are you apologizing to me for? I'm used to your wild sleeping. I just want to make sure you are okay."

Candy moved the hair away from Hazel's face and planted an icy kiss on her cheek. Hazel managed a weak smile.

"Yeah. I'm okay. What about you?"

Candy waved nonchalantly, dreamily, staring up at the ceiling.

"I'm always okay, doll."

A text message sound chimed from her phone that was laying beside her on the side table. She pulled her eyes away from Candy and grabbed her phone, using her face to unlock the screen. Tate's message sent her heart into her stomach. Her pulse quickened.

"I spoke to Detective Bourgeois, and he agreed to meet with you at 11 a.m. today. Let me know if that's okay."

Another text flitted across the screen just as she was reading the first. "Oh... and thanks for an amazing night. I love you."

Her previously sunk heart fluttered as she thought about the passion she and Tate shared from the night before. The high she went to bed on was nearly enough to float her through the week, if not for the potential meeting with a police detective. Hazel was already debilitatingly introverted and protective of her secret abilities. She knew it was her idea to get involved with the investigation of the abduction and murder of those women, but that did not make it any easier for her to swallow.

"Are you going to go?" Candy asked, tearing Hazel out of her own head.

Hazel shrugged, but she knew the answer. After everything she had seen in the memories of the victims, she had to go. She had to get involved in a bigger way. Just watching the memories unfold in her mind would not locate the missing Michelle Barrilleaux or find the killer of the other three women.

"I guess I have to go, but that doesn't make it any easier to make the leap. I mean, what if the detective thinks I'm crazy?"

"You are crazy." Candy smirked, pulling her spectral form closer to Hazel until their shoulders were touching. Hazel shivered and pulled her blankets to her chin. "I'm joking, obviously. He won't think you're crazy. Even if he's not a believer, the police department can use any help they can get, and what you've seen so far with undoubtedly help them. He'd be a fool not to listen to what you have to say. Plus, I'm sure Tate would have briefed him on your abilities. He wouldn't throw you in there blind."

Hazel nodded, but was not convinced. Her ever present self-doubt ensured that. Reopening the screen of her phone, she responded to Tate's message. She sent heart emojis in response to his loving mention of their previous night, and agreed to meet with the detective, although she expressed her hesitancy. He assured her she had nothing to worry about and told her to message him after the meeting.

***

Entering the police department to meet with Detective Bourgeois, Hazel's heart was beating a million miles per minute. Tate assured her that the detective was open to her abilities, but she was unsure. The last thing she wanted was to become a laughingstock of the department, especially with it being Tate's workplace. After meeting with Samantha Bourgeois to rent her apartment, she knew the detective's wife at least partly believed in spirits, but she did not know how far that belief went. There were several moments, while she waited in the lobby for the detective to be available, where she thought about heading for the exit and forgetting the entire plan. But she reminded herself of why she was there, to help the murder victims who kept coming to her, and that was something she could not ignore.

Before she had the chance to question her plan one last time, a tall man with dirty blond hair and bright blue eyes approached her with his hand held out for a handshake. He looked at her curiously, as though he had been standing there for longer than she realized. Standing up awkwardly, she tried to shake his hand in a more professional manner than she felt comfortable with.

"Hazel Watson, I presume?"

She nodded as she swallowed back the self-doubt ever present in her mind, only remembering to speak after a few awkward moments. "Yes. Thank you for seeing me."

He smiled warmly, disarming her only slightly. Detective Bourgeois was at least ten years older than her and Tate, but he was quite handsome. She thought, for a moment, that she was glad she had left Candy at home, because Candy's invisible flirting would have created an impossible distraction.

"Don't mention it. I've been wanting to meet the woman who stole Tate Cormier's heart." He motioned towards the hallway towards the back of the lobby. "Follow me to my office."

She nodded, following the detective to the back part of the building. Just like her old office in the Public Defender's building, the police precinct held more than living souls. She kept her eyes down to refrain from locking eyes with the resident ghosts, since she could not handle any more than she already had haunting her, but she could see their spectral forms in her peripheral vision. Detective Bourgeois checked the hall before shutting the door behind them. When he sat at his desk, his expression became more somber than it had been in the lobby.

"So...," he hesitated. "I hate to jump right in, but with the handful of women who have already fallen victim to someone who still remains at large, I feel like I don't have much time to waste. I'm not sure how you refer to what you do, but Tate explained you to be... I'm guessing clairvoyant?"

The jumble of words that had fallen out of his mouth caught her off guard. Maybe it was because her anxiety was at an all-time high, but she found the entire scene difficult to process. She had never thought of herself as clairvoyant. It always seemed like a title people on television would use for someone else. Her family had never referred to it by any specific title. It was just an ability she was born with. Realizing the awkward silences were not helping her case, she did her best to pull herself out of her head.

"I've never given it a name... but if you're referring to my ability to communicate with the dead... then yes. I do have that ability." She paused, fumbling with the ring of keys in her hand. "I'm sorry. I'm not used to talking about this with people, but I felt like I had to get involved. These women..." She discreetly wiped a tear from her eye. The situation had become overwhelming to her. She wanted to seem in control, but she was losing that fight. "These women have been coming to me... all except Michelle. I haven't seen her yet and I'm hoping there is still time to find her. I would have never made the choice to come out with my abilities if it weren't for the possibility that we could find Michelle before it was too late."

He nodded. His face relaxed as warmth flooded his eyes. He knew she was having a hard time being there, talking about her abilities, and he wanted to make it easier on her.

He believes me.

"Miss Watson, the usefulness of psychics in police investigations may be controversial, but psychics have long been and will undoubtedly continue to be involved in criminal investigations. I know, for a fact, that Tate Cormier wouldn't be about to marry a fraud. I also know what my wife experienced in that apartment you decided to move into after so many people ran away from it screaming." He paused, eyeing her inquisitively. "The apartment Candy Townsend was murdered in. I have it on good authority that Candy's spirit remained in that apartment, and you moved in because you could communicate with her... that's why you didn't run scared from that apartment."

She could not hide the shock in her eyes when she realized he saw her for who she was. She had not told him about Candy, but he knew. Even though he suspected, she found it hard to confirm his suspicions.

"Miss Watson..."

"I'm sorry. Like I said before, it's just hard for me to talk about this, but yes, you are correct. I called your wife about the apartment because I overheard some girls in a coffee shop talking about how it was haunted and vacant. I wasn't particularly looking for a haunted place to live. Goodness knows Candy is a handful." She could not help but to roll her eyes when she thought about her spunky best friend. "But I needed a place to live, and I knew I could get a good price for a haunted apartment where no one else wanted to live. Candy was still there, and apparently tormenting your wife, and anyone else who tried to move in there."

The detective chuckled as well, lightening the

mood even more. "I also heard the apartment was easier to show since you moved out. Can I assume Candy left when you did?"

Once again, the detective figured it out. It was his job, though, so she was not surprised. "Yeah... she left and moved in with me and Tate."

The detective's eyes showed his amusement. "Well, that is a story I need to hear more about. I hear Candy was quite a fun lady. It's so sad what happened to her."

Hazel nodded, feeling the emotions tug at her at the thought of what happened to Candy.

"Yeah... well, she's making the best of her situation."

The detective's mood shifted. Hazel thought he may have remembered his obligations.

"So... you said you have been visited by all the victims except Michelle. Have they told you anything about the killer?"

"Not really... all I've been told is he wore a mask. Actually... Emily thought he was a swamp monster." She glanced up at him. "She really thought it was an actual swamp monster."

His eyebrows furrowed as he appeared to ponder the thought. He shuffled through the paperwork on his desk and separated a piece of paper from the stack, showing it to Hazel. Her stomach clenched as she stared at the image.

"Is this what she saw?" he asked.

The picture suspended in front of her was the sketch of a monster. A monster she had only ever seen in her dreams. The details on the page shocked her. Seven feet tall. Three hundred pounds. Haunting yellow eyes framed by shaggy gray hair stared back at her.

"There are many stories about this creature," he said. "The stories date back to before the Acadians arrived on this land. Now, frankly, I'm not a believer. I think these stories are based on a man in a realistic costume. But costume or not, this person has camouflaged himself enough to fool many people. I'm guessing someone is taking advantage of this legend to hunt for victims. Either way, we need to catch him. I'm hoping you can help me with that."

She nodded, taking the sketch from him and examining it more closely.

"I'm assuming this came from a witness?"

"Yes... Emily Landry, actually. This sketch was created after her first report of the creature near her backyard. Within a week, she was missing. Normally, we would discount such a claim, but she isn't the only one to have seen it recently."

Taking one more cursory glance at the sketch, she handed it back to the detective.

"I wish I knew more about him. All I know from speaking to Malerie and Emily is that their killer wore a mask. They did not see his face. But..." she hesitated, unsure how well-received what she had to say would be. "My abilities work in many ways, but I'm unsure how to explain what I'm trying to say. You see... speaking to spirits is not the only way I can communicate with them."

His eyes were unblinking as he seemed to hang on her every word. She continued.

"Sometimes... actually, oftentimes... they invade my dreams to show me scenes from their memories. It's how... it's how I helped to discover what happened to many spirits, including Candy."

"So, you see their experiences in your dreams?" he asked.

"Yes, although it's not always scenes they want me to see. Sometimes it seems to be unintentional, like their memories transfer without their knowledge. But otherwise... Anyway... Emily says she saw a swamp monster, but I have seen the killer, or at least who I expect is the killer, in another memory that was sent to me by Malerie. I received the memory from her weeks ago, before Harmony Richard was arrested. In the scene I saw then, the killer wasn't recognizable, but he drove a car."

His eyes opened wide. What she said seemed to catch him by surprise.

"When I saw the scene play out, and I saw the killer in shadow, I didn't get the feeling he was a monster. I believed him to be a man. I don't know a lot about Louisiana swamp monsters, Detective Bourgeois, but I don't think they can drive."

The office had gotten quiet enough to hear a pin drop for several agonizing moments while Hazel sat quietly, waiting for him to absorb her story, and hoping nothing she said would have caused him to doubt her. He pulled a notepad out of his top desk drawer, opening it to a clean page before setting his eyes back on her.

"Do you remember the color of the vehicle?

The make or model? Anything about it would help."

Hazel had never thought much about the car. In the nightmare, she was tied up. Being abducted and trapped in a trunk next to the body of a dead woman left little time to examine the vehicle properly. She bit her lip.

"I couldn't see much from my vantage point, but it was definitely a sedan. One with a large trunk. In the nightmare, I was a victim of abduction as well. I was tied up next to Malerie's body. It was big enough to fit both of us in it."

He nodded as he scribbled onto his pad of paper, although she did not feel like she had given him anything helpful.

"And the height of the man... how tall would you say he was?"

"Tall... I mean very tall. I didn't see his face, but I saw him in that nightmare I mentioned before... the one with him in shadow, but I have seen him in other dreams as well. I've seen him when dressed in his swamp monster suit several times. I'd say at least three times, maybe more... If it's the same person. Emily wasn't exaggerating about his height. He was at least six and a half feet, unless his boots made him taller. I wasn't close enough to tell."

He continued to scribble, barely glancing up at her as she sat across from him. She almost felt like she was in the principal's office and had gotten into trouble, or at least she believed that was what it would have felt like.

"Anything else you can tell me about what happened to the victims? Where he kept them or anything along those lines?"

For the first time since seeing Malerie's spirit outside of her apartment building, Hazel had begun to feel useful, because she had seen more than she previously realized. Finally, she was able to tell the police things that only her abilities allowed her to know. She realized it was a huge responsibility, but she still felt the release of getting it off of her chest.

"I don't know exactly where he kept them, but I have seen the inside of the structure in visions. It's some sort of..." She thought for a moment, unsure exactly what the structure was called. "I guess I'd best describe it as a wooden shed or a shack. There isn't much to it. It's small. I didn't even see a bathroom. The women have a bucket on the floor. The windows are barred. He doesn't even tie them up because they cannot escape. There are too many locks on the door. Oh... and I think he drugs them."

Recounting the vision brought feelings of dread to her chest, making the air seem thinner. She looked to the floor and tried to ground herself. The emotions flooding into her seemed denser than she expected, even discussing such a difficult subject. The room grew cold as the realization hit her. They were no longer alone.

"Miss Watson, are you okay?"

She heard his words, but she was too afraid to look up, too afraid to lock eyes with a spirit who would undoubtedly follow her home.

"I'll get you some water. I'll be right back."

He went to get up from his desk, but she grabbed his arm, slightly harder than she intended. She started to feel the tears drip from her eyes as she stared at the floor. "Please don't leave me alone in here."

He gingerly lowered himself back into his chair. Releasing his arm, she pulled her hands back into a ball in her lap.

"Do you need for me to call Tate? Is there something I can do for you right now?"

She shook her head, angrily wiping the moisture from her cheek.

"Tate can't help me with this. I don't want to freak you out, but I don't think we are alone anymore."

She could feel his fear build up and she knew he was probably frantically scanning the room but coming up empty. The only person who could see them was her, and she would have to face the spirit, eventually. He lowered himself from his chair until he was nearly on his knees, bringing his line of sight to meet hers. She closed her eyes tightly, shying away from him seeing her in such an emotional state. His voice came out near a whisper when he spoke.

"Who is here with us, Miss Watson?"

Wiping her cheeks one last time, she finally raised her eyes to scan the room, flinching when her gaze landed upon Emily Landry's ghostly face, standing just behind the detective's desk.

The spirit of Emily reflected the pain Hazel felt deep within her bones. Sorrow Hazel had no right to feel. Her eyes held a longing Hazel knew she could never fill because she could not bring her back. She could not bring her back to her little girl. Hazel looked back at the detective, who was still kneeling on the floor in front of her.

"It's Emily Landry. She's standing behind you."

His eyes revealed terror, but she could tell he was trying to mask it. He did not dare to turn and look behind himself, not that he could have seen her, anyway.

"Okay. Okay. Do you have any idea what she wants from us? Is there a way for her to help us help her?"

Hazel did not have much hope for Emily to be of any help. It was not that Emily's spirit did not want to help, but she didn't remember much that was helpful. At least not the last time she appeared to Hazel. Still, even though she did not feel optimistic, Hazel returned her eyes to Emily, hoping for an answer to the detective's question.

The spirit dashed forward, somehow fitting her form between Hazel and Detective Bourgeois. Her eyes were wild and desperate. Hazel flinched at what felt like an incoming assault.

"It's Joshua!" Emily cried. "He's going to get himself killed! Please help him!"

Hazel nodded vigorously before standing up quickly, grabbing her satchel from the floor. The detective watched her in surprise.

"It's her husband. She said he's up to something, and he's going to get himself killed. We have to go!"

Detective Bourgeois did not ask any questions. He nodded, grabbed his hat off his desk, and ran for the door. "Let's go!"

***

Climbing into the detective's vehicle, Hazel sent a quick text message to Tate, letting him know what was going on.

"Tate asked if he should meet us at the Landry's home. What should I tell him?"

"I'd tell him to meet us there. We may need backup."

Hazel nodded and relayed the message, although she did not like the idea of Tate meeting them there. She knew it was his job, but she would never get used to him working in a field that put him in so much danger, even if it was to protect her.

11

Vigilance

The drive to the Honey Island area was painfully slow. Even with police lights and sirens on, there were areas of New Orleans where the traffic allowed little flexibility for even emergency vehicles to pass. Detective Bourgeois got onto his radio and called for an officer closer to the area, asking them to stop by the Landry's home, but none of them had any idea what they would find when they got there, or if Joshua Landry was even at home. Hazel glanced into the backseat, as had become a habit, to see that Emily was not there. She imagined the spirit had returned to her husband's side, powerless to stop whatever it was he was doing. Hazel couldn't imagine what that would be.

When they finally arrived at the home, another police officer was already there and was walking around the yard with his weapon in hand. There was no evidence Joshua was there. The house was quiet. Almost too quiet. Heaviness in her chest slowed her paces as she walked. In her peripheral vision, she glimpsed Emily's spirit going around to the backyard. Hazel followed, calling the detective after her. When she made it around the back of the house, she could see Emily's spirit hovering near the bank of the canal, which separated her yard from the swamp. Emily pointed into the distance. Hazel closed the distance between them, trying to see what it was Emily was pointing at, but all she saw was trees.

"He's in there," Emily said. "He has a gun."

Relaying Emily's message to Detective Bourgeois and the other officer, both men rushed to the small bridge crossing the water and disappeared into the swamp, but not before ordering Hazel to stay where she was. Emily disappeared, undoubtedly following the officers.

Leaving the bank of the canal, she walked a few yards closer to the house and sat on the bench near the back door. Time seemed to stand still as she waited until a third police car and two ambulances drove up and parked near the side of the house. Her heart leaped as Tate jumped out of it and ran to her, grabbing her up from the bench and checking her to make sure she was not harmed.

"Are you okay? Where is the detective? What's going on?" Tate squeezed her as though he hadn't seen her in ages, and it worked to release some of the stress coursing through her body.

"I'm not sure what's going on. Emily said her husband was in the swamp. Detective Bourgeois and the other officer ran in there but ordered me to stay here."

He stared into the distance, hugging her tightly and kissing the top of her head.

"I need to go in after them. Please stay here."

He tried to pull away, but she refused to let go of him.

"No way, Tate." She looked into his eyes as she held her arms around him. "I just almost lost you, and her husband has a gun. They all have guns, and no one is expecting you out there. I will not have you get shot. I know it's your job, but not today. Today, your job is to be my fiancé. I'm not letting you go. Please don't make me."

She felt his body release as he nodded and kissed her, although he kept returning his stare to the tree line. Wrapping his arm around her, he led her to his police car, opening the door for her to get inside.

"Why are we getting into your car?"

"If someone shoots, I'd rather there be something solid protecting you. Don't worry. I'll get in with you. I'm going to call for backup."

She nodded and hesitantly stepped into the car, allowing Tate to close the door behind her. Part of her expected him to run towards the swamp, but he did not. Instead, he walked around to his side of the car and climbed inside. Pulling his radio handset to his mouth, he contacted dispatch for backup, and updated them on what was going on. They assured him that more units were on the way. Hazel breathed a sigh of relief as she gazed out of the window, waiting to see movement in the distance.

They sat in Tate's car for about ten minutes before other police cars began pulling up. Once other officers arrived, Tate got out of the car to speak to them, but he asked Hazel to stay inside the car where it was safe. Part of her wanted to argue, but she obliged. After a brief conversation, four of the other officers headed towards the bridge and crossed into the swamp, heading in the same direction where the detective and the other officer had gone before.

Tate returned to his spot beside her in the car, reaching over to grab her hand as he sat back down.

"Any idea what's going on?" she asked, although she did not expect he had the answer.

"No one has any idea what's going on, actually. They've been in contact with Joshua Landry's mother. She said he dropped off his daughter at her house this morning, but she hasn't heard from him since then and no one else seems to know where he is. They are trying to get in touch with his friend, Hunter, but have been unable to so far. His mom confirmed that he owns a twelve-gauge shotgun. Which isn't good, if that's what he has in there with him right now. I would hate for anyone to get shot by a gun like that. But no one seems to know what brought him into those woods in the first place or what he went in after."

An icy dread expanded in Hazel's core as she stared out of the window, hoping she would see all the living people return from the swamp unharmed.

"I just wish I knew what was going on. Emily seemed frantic when she came to me in the precinct. Wait... what's that?"

Seeing movement in the distance, Hazel went to open the door, but Tate's hand shot out in front of her, stopping her from getting out of the car.

"Hang on, sweetie. We need to make sure it's safe first."

She nodded and sat back in her seat while her eyes were focused on the tree-line where she could see several men meandering through the trees towards her direction. One officer held his arm, which was bleeding, while the detective held onto a man in handcuffs. But he was not

Joshua Landry. Noticing what she was seeing, Tate darted out of the car to help the wounded officer. Hazel continued to watch, hoping to see Joshua or Emily, but not seeing them anywhere.

The man in handcuffs was tall and ragged, like he hadn't had a haircut or a shave in a while. Another officer had a gun slung over his shoulder while he helped to escort the tall man. Hazel assumed it was the handcuffed man's weapon. Approaching the injured officer, Tate wrapped a rag around the man's bleeding arm and led him to the waiting ambulance while they talked. Hazel wished she could know what they were talking about, wished she had some update as to what had come of Joshua, but she waited.

A few more officers followed behind the first group, and she could finally see Joshua Landry, also in handcuffs, being escorted by two officers. A shotgun was draped over the shoulder of one of those officers as well. Once she saw that all men with guns were under control, she felt it was safe to get out of the car. She needed to know what was going on.

Hazel approached Detective Bourgeois. He had just handed the large man over to another officer, who was putting the prisoner in the back of a police car. Noticing Hazel approaching, the detective turned around to face her.

"Are you okay, Miss Watson? You stayed here like I told you to, right? It wasn't safe out there."

She nodded her head before pointing at the large man who had just been loaded into the back of a police car. "Who is that guy?"

The detective looked back at the police car, pointing at the same man. "Who? That big guy?"

Hazel nodded.

"His name is Hunter Billiot. He just got out of a few days in jail from a bar fight, so I don't know why he's testing his luck. I believe he and Joshua are friends. He got freaked out when we approached and his damn gun discharged, shooting Lawson over there. He'll be okay, though. It could have been worse."

"Well, I'm glad he's going to be okay. Any idea why Joshua Landry and his friend were in the swamp wielding guns in the first place?"

"From what we gathered, Joshua was tired of us not finding his wife's killer, so he was going to take the law into his own hands." The detective, who usually kept his face passive of emotion, let a smirk slide across it.

"Like a vigilante? That's what he was trying to do?"

The detective's response came out snarkier than she expected when he said, "Yep."

"Wow. I can't believe they thought that was okay. So, what's going to happen to them?"

The detective shrugged before answering. "Well, Hunter shot an officer, but it was an accident. I'm going to have to think about how I want to handle this, especially with Joshua. I need to scare him enough to where he doesn't pull anything like that again, but I have no intention of taking him away from his little girl. She's already lost her mom. Well, Miss Watson, I suspect we will be in touch some more but, for now, why don't you head back home with Tate. Y'all keep each other safe now." He smiled, touched her arm gently, and walked away. Tate was still deep in conversation, but Hazel saw Emily near the swing set, so she approached the spirit, hoping Emily had more information to help the case.

Emily turned to face her, smiling gently.

"Thank you for coming here and helping my husband."

"You're welcome. I wish I could do more."

Emily nodded, moving in closer to Hazel. "I want to show you something," she said as she reached out and placed both of her hands on the sides of Hazel's face. The sensation was icy cold before everything went dark.

***

The morning air was cool, definitely more pleasant than it would be once the sun rose to the top of the sky. It had been over a week since I had seen the creature in the swamp, but the police assured me they would monitor the area for illegal hunting. My flowerbed would not plant itself. So, before the air felt like a sauna, I called to Bella, and we headed into the backyard for some much-needed fresh air.

Bella excitedly ran in circles in the grass, nearly making me dizzy. I stumbled back, watching the glee on her face. "Mommy! Can you push me on the swing?"

"Race you to it!" I said as I gave Bella a head start to the swing set in the opposite direction of my

flowerbed. I had to get my flowers planted, but playing with Bella would have to come first.

Bella awkwardly climbed into the swing lowest to the ground. Joshua and I bought her a big girl swing set for Christmas, but she was petite for seven years old and could barely lift herself into the seats. She would surely be tall enough before we knew it.

My yard was one of my prized possessions. Having bounced around apartment complexes as a child, giving my daughter a backyard she could play in was important to me. With the new swing set and her princess playhouse, I can live vicariously through Bella. Watching her play has always given me so much joy. I giggled as her legs swung back and forth with the motion, unable to touch the ground.

My smile faltered when my eyes betrayed me, leaving the joyous vision of Bella swinging back and forth in front of me and instead roaming the swamp that laid across the small canal lining my back yard. A cool breeze seemed to flow across only me, making my skin prickle. I was assured there would be no hunters in those trees, no swamp monsters looking for prey, but I couldn't help but feel the eyes watching us. A flock of birds took flight as the trees rustled.

"What do you say we go inside and bake some cookies?"

Bella jumped off the swing before it was parallel to the ground. I lurched forward and tried to soften her landing, but she seemed unphased by the impact.

"Yay! I want some cookies!"

Turning my eyes away from the trees, I chased behind Bella as she ran towards the door. My flowers would have to wait until Joshua got home. My heart broke because my backyard no longer felt safe, but I couldn't shake the ominous feeling that had overcome me. I hoped it would pass as I locked the door behind us.

***

"Hazel! Oh no! Hazel!"

Hazel awoke to the feeling of her body being lifted off the ground and carried quickly, but she did not know to where. Her head was fuzzy as she struggled to open her eyes. Tate was carrying her, running with her towards the ambulances and police cars that remained on the property.

His running slowed when he noticed she was awake and he kneeled with her, placing her gently on his lap.

"Tate... what's going on?" She still felt dazed. He squeezed her softly before kissing her on the head. His eyes were brimming with emotion.

"I saw you sprawled out on the ground in the backyard and I panicked. I thought you were hurt." Wiping tears from his cheek, he pulled her into his neck. She could feel his body tremble underneath her. He was scared, something she promised never to do to him again, but she didn't even know what happened.

They were halfway between the place where she had fallen and the collection of emergency vehicles that remained after the earlier incident. One officer caught sight of them on the ground and began running over to help.

"I went to the swing set because I saw Emily." She fought her lightheadedness, wrapping her hand around Tate's arm to ground herself. "She touched my face... and everything went black."

Tate's eyebrows drew together as he caressed her cheek. The electricity from his touch sent goosebumps down her body. She looked into his eyes, temporarily lost in the moment. "She caused you to black out?"

"Not exactly," she muttered, almost scared to

tell him about the advanced nature of her interaction with Emily. "She sent a memory to me... which never happened to me while awake." She shook her head, still not understanding how it all worked. "I don't understand how it happened. One minute I was lucid and awake and the next minute I was dreaming her memory."

Just as she finished explaining, the other officer, an older man, approached them, panting from his jog.

"Is she okay? Do you need a stretcher?" he asked, kneeling down near Hazel's side.

Tate glanced down at her, and she shook her head. The dizziness had passed, and she did not want the police fussing over her when someone else had been shot. She could walk. Tate returned his eyes to the other officer.

"No. I think she's okay now. She just got lightheaded from not eating."

With his arms still wrapped around her, Tate helped her to her feet. "Come on, love. Let's go get you something to eat."

Tate returned one last glance to the other

officer. "Thank you for your help, Mitchell. I'm going to get her out of here."

The middle-aged officer nodded, smiling kindly before walking back to the shrinking crowd near the side of the house.

Detective Bourgeois was still standing near the group of officers. He smiled at them as they approached Tate's car to leave. The ambulance with the injured Officer Lawson had already left, as had the police cruisers containing Joshua Landry and his friend. Hazel wondered what charges the men would receive for their vigilante hunt in the swamp, but she hoped, at least for Emily's young daughter, Bella, that her father would be home quickly. She wished she could speak to Joshua, and tell him Emily was around and watching, but enough people already knew about her abilities, so she resigned herself to operating in the background.

Closing her into the car, Tate climbed into his own seat and turned to face her.

"Are you hungry?"

"Yes, but would it be okay if we just grabbed something to go? I think I'm ready to go home."

He leaned over to kiss her before putting the

vehicle in reverse. "Of course. I'm honestly ready to go home as well."

12

Visitors

The sky was still dark when Hazel woke to pain all over her body. It was not a common occurrence to wake up in physical pain, but she thought it could have been from her fall in the Landry's yard. Tate had fussed over her for the entire night after they got home from the ordeal, running her bath, cooking her dinner, and refusing to let her go as they fell asleep. His arm still draped across her stomach when the aches woke her. Although she expected spirits to be there when she woke, she was relieved when she did not see any in their bedroom.

She thought about what happened the night before, how Emily had transferred a memory to her while she was wide awake, causing her to lose consciousness. She had never experienced anything like that. Never thought it was possible. Emily's spirit had always seemed so weak, so Hazel did not understand how she found the ability to test Hazel's abilities in such a way? However, she did it, Hazel hoped she would not do it again, and planned to tell Emily just that. Spirits rarely considered her feelings, but she hoped this one would.

Tate had not brought the incident up again after they left the Landry's house, probably because he realized it was hard enough for her to cope with, without dredging it up repeatedly. She appreciated his ability to drop conversations when he knew they were difficult for her.

Doing her best to forget about what happened by the swing set, if even for a few hours, Hazel closed her eyes and attempted to fall back asleep.

***

When Hazel awoke the second time, she was alone in the bed, but she could see the bathroom light shining from beneath the door. Checking the clock on the bedside table, she realized Tate must have been getting ready for work. She sighed. Being what amounted to a homemaker was going to take some getting used to. Maybe she could take some cooking classes, something to help pass the time and make her more useful, make her a more fitting spouse for Tate.

Tate stepped out of the bathroom quietly, clearly trying to not wake her up, but he smiled when he saw she was awake. Already dressed in his uniform, he looked amazing, although it took little for him to look good.

"Sorry," he whispered. "Did I wake you?"

She shook her head. "No. I woke up a few minutes ago."

He moved across the room and sat down on the bed next to her, kissing her gently. "So, what's on your agenda for today."

"I think I'm going to reach back out to Hera.

She asked to spend time together, so she could reconnect with Candy."

He nodded, reaching down to hold her hand. "That's a good idea. I'll be home around dinnertime. Do you want me to bring something home?"

"You don't have to. I can take care of dinner. It's the least I can do after all you do to take care of me."

"You don't have to worry about that. I love taking care of you. I'll see you later." He gave her one last kiss and left for work.

Closing her eyes and preparing her mind for the day, Hazel grabbed her cellphone and offered to meet with Hera again. She did not expect a response as quickly as she received one. Off for the day, because of a doctor's appointment, Hera offered to come by their house around lunchtime. Although not completely ready for company, Hazel climbed off the bed and headed to share the news with Candy.

Expecting to find Candy in her new bedroom, Hazel was startled when she saw Candy's spectral form in the kitchen, looking out the window.

"Damn, Candy! You scared me half to death!"

Candy turned around, just as startled.

"I'm sorry, doll. I didn't mean to scare you. I was just watching the storm clouds. Looks like it's going to be a bad one."

Joining her friend at the window, Hazel looked outside. Candy was right about the clouds. Black clouds billowing in the sky threatened a monster of a storm.

"Wow, yeah. Hopefully, it doesn't prevent Hera from coming over. Maybe I should offer her a raincheck. No pun intended. I don't want her to get into an accident coming out here."

Candy gazed out of the window for a quiet moment. Hazel watched her eyes, which always resembled that of a child when she watched storms, like there was magic in it. She wondered if Candy had always been fascinated by storms, even before she died, but she never asked. The life in Candy's eyes when she gazed into something exciting warmed Hazel's heart.

"I don't know, Hazel. Maybe it'll pass before she heads this way. I'd say give it some time."

"Okay. In the meantime, after I get cleaned up,

I have a vital task for you. It's a matter of national security."

Hazel tried to keep her face serious, but Candy lifted a comical eyebrow at her, causing her facade to crack. She could hide nothing from Candy, and she knew it.

"And what task is that?"

Hazel smirked, opening the refrigerator to grab the coffee creamer. "Dinner."

As Hazel expected, Candy let out a laugh. "Dinner?" Candy approached her, reaching out to tame Hazel's tousled hair. "I guess it would be serious if Tate cared about that kind of stuff. But..." She sighed dramatically. "I get why you want to learn. It's not a bad skill to hone. I'm not so bad at it, myself."

Hazel scoffed. "Well then, Betty Crocker, how about you help a girl out? Hopefully, we can make something decent with the food already in this house because I do not want to drive in that storm."

Glancing back out the window, Hazel could see the storm had grown closer, and was about to unleash hell on her house. Unlike Candy, severe storms scared her. She had seen the devastation they could bring, and, unlike Candy, she could still be affected by it.

Stepping to the refrigerator, Candy motioned for Hazel to open its door. "Come on, well. Let's see what the two of you mortals have for ingredients."

As Hazel opened the refrigerator door, she was glad Tate had the habit of stopping by the grocery store. If it had been her apartment fridge, she knew it would undoubtedly be empty.

Peering into the refrigerator as though she were solving a scientific hypothesis, Candy twirled her hair thoughtfully. "Good thing your man actually shops for groceries."

"Yeah. I was just thinking the same thing. So... is anything in there usable?"

Candy floated to the pantry door, which she traversed through as though it was not there, popping back out only seconds after she entered.

"Well... there's nothing spectacular in here... but you can throw together pasta for him. It is, after all, one of the easiest things to make if you have only a handful of ingredients. He has some veggie meat, a few vegetables, pasta sauce and dried pasta. That's pretty easy to throw together, and doesn't take much time to do so."

"That's great! It's a start at least. I should probably take a cooking class or something, though. I hate that he always feels the need to buy takeout for us. It is definitely on my list of priorities."

Exiting the pantry, Candy hopped onto the counter, swinging her legs playfully from side to side. "I guess I'd even fund that. I do like my new bedroom and would prefer you keep the man, not that he'd leave you for starving him. Hey... it would probably be fun... and you need more fun."

Hazel rolled her eyes at the insinuation. "I have fun... sometimes."

"Sure, you do, doll. Sure, you do."

Hazel stuck out her tongue at Candy before leaving the kitchen and heading to the bedroom so she could get dressed for the day. Although she would have preferred to spend her days in pajamas since she no longer had to appear in court, she thought letting herself become too lax would be bad for her motivation.

The news threatened a tornado warning, but

the worse they got was a lot of rain and flickering lights. After a few hours of threats, the thunderstorm passed with no lasting damage. Hera texted, letting Hazel know she was on her way, making Hazel's nerves wind up into a coil. Candy was excited to see her old friend, but Hazel was not comfortable entertaining anyone.

When Hera rang the doorbell, Candy got to the door before Hazel had, and was so excited that Hazel could not help but to let her guard down. Candy deserved a little joy in her afterlife. The sky still threatened a storm, but the rain had stopped for the time being.

"Hey Hazel," Hera said as she set her umbrella against the front porch. "I almost thought I was going to have to give you a raincheck with this storm, but I'm glad it calmed down out here."

Hazel forced a smile, still feeling uncomfortable hanging out with someone she did not really know. Candy nudged her. "Yeah. That weather was crazy. Come on inside where it's dry," she said as she backed out of the doorway and into the house. Hera followed her, kicking off her shoes in the foyer before following Hazel into the kitchen.

"Coffee?"

"Thank you, Hazel. That would be great."

Short on words, as was often the case, Hazel busied herself with making the coffee while Hera sat down at the table.

"Is Candy here?"

Hazel turned to look at the red-headed spirit behind her before answering. "Oh, yeah. She usually is. She's sitting next to you at the table. She is really excited to see you."

Hera smiled, looking towards the empty chair next to her. She reached her hand to the space in front of the chair and spoke to Candy, although she could not see her. "I'm excited to be here with you too, Candy. I've missed you."

Hazel glanced behind her to see Candy smiling ear to ear, holding Hera's hand, although Hera didn't realize it. Hazel grabbed the coffee cups, cream and sugar, placed everything onto the table and sat down as well. "Do you feel her holding your hand? It would probably feel cold, and maybe a bit electric."

Hera stared down at her hand for several moments before looking back at Hazel. "She's holding my hand right now?"

"Yes."

"I do feel something, but I'd hate to think it's only because of the power of suggestion."

"She is holding your hand, but not everyone can feel a spirit's touch. If there is anything you want to say to her, she can hear you. I'd be happy to leave the two of you alone if you'd feel better talking to her without me here. You would just need me to tell you any of her responses. It's completely up to you."

Hera reached her other hand across the table and grabbed Hazel's. "You don't have to leave the room for me to talk to Candy. Hazel, this is your house. Anything I have to say to Candy, I can say to you. Plus, like you said, I need you to tell me her responses, anyway. I just appreciate you doing this for us... more than you'll ever know."

Hazel nodded, taking a sip of her coffee while Hera fixed hers with cream and sugar.

"Tell Hera that her fiancé is hot," Candy said. Her chin was propped on top of folded hands as she stared dreamily at Hera.

Hazel snickered and then relayed the message. Hera chuckled as well.

"That sounds exactly like something Candy

would say. I'm glad she hasn't changed, well, her personality anyway. And yes, Adele is hot. Thank you."

Hazel could tell Hera had thought about Candy's death and it dampened her mood. Her eyes had become glassy.

"Yeah. She can be a handful, especially before she and Jake got reconnected. Although the circumstances were unfortunate. I know Candy loves having him around and being able to touch him again. Before that, she would flirt with my man pretty continuously. She still sometimes tries to catch him naked, though." Hazel laughed, causing Hera to laugh as well.

"Oh, man. I can't imagine. So, she and Jake can have... like... a sex life?" Hera sounded incredulous. Her eyebrows arched.

Hazel looked at Candy before answering the question. "Well, they couldn't at first. Jake had a hard time... controlling his energy right after he died, so he would disappear without warning to build his energy back up. After a few months, however, of him coming and going, he's learned to control his energy much better, so he is with Candy more often. From what I've been told, they have found ways to be together sexually, even under such circumstances."

"Thank goodness," Candy sighed. "I could still go for more loving, though. We will get there, hopefully."

"Candy just said she could use some more loving, but thinks it will improve with time."

Hera smiled, wiping a tear from her eye. "I don't know if I'm supposed to be sad about Jake or happy he is with her now. My emotions have been all over the place."

Hazel nodded. "I know exactly what you mean. Candy does too. We've all felt the exact same way. I can say, at least for now, that she and Jake don't dwell on the past. It's not beneficial to dwell on things you can't change. They focus on what they have now... on what makes a difference to them now."

Hera nodded, still holding Hazel's hand from across the table.

"Candy always was an optimist."

"She still is."

After a visit lasting an hour, Hera ended up heading home. Hazel felt proud of herself for meeting up with Hera for a second time, because it was usually unlike her to meet with people in social situations, especially people she did not know personally. She would do anything for Candy, however, so she planned another meetup with Hera soon.

13

Return to the Scene

"They're doing nothing to find my wife's killer. We can't allow a killer to hunt for innocent women in our community! We have to band together and do what the police don't have the guts to do! We have to hunt him down!"

Joshua Landry's eyes were wild as the local news interviewed him from the steps of the city jail. He had been released that morning, and word spread like wildfire about what he was doing in the swamp the day before. He was hunting for his wife's killer, and it appeared the locals were on his side. Every bit of concrete outside the doors of the jail was crawling with people leading up to his release. In less than twenty-four hours since his arrest, he had amassed hundreds of supporters.

Joshua's friend, Hunter, had yet to be released, however. Apparently, shooting a police officer, even if it was accidental, was not as easy to forgive. There were so many people surrounding the entrance to the jail that police had to escort Joshua out of the city, but not before he got on live television and threw the police department under the metaphorical bus.

Hazel and Tate watched the news broadcast from the living room sofa. Having watched as Mr. Landry's car drove away from the police station, Tate lowered the volume of the television before turning to Hazel.

"Wow. This is not good," he said. "What happened to his wife is messed up, and I understand it can't be easy to be in his shoes and have to wait while this killer is at large, but I don't think him going up against the police department is going to help him or the victims."

Tate's face was set in harder lines than Hazel was used to seeing him. She thought he was more worried than angry, but it all showed on his face. He took his job seriously, making it extra painful to be treated like they were not doing all they could do for a victim. Hazel also knew how important solving this case was to the department. They were desperate enough to find this predator that they pursued help from someone like her. She reached over and touched his face, pulling him forward until their lips touched. The tension in his body released before she allowed herself to pull away.

"I agree with you, baby. Don't take what he's doing personally. I hope what he is saying doesn't rowdy up people against the police department. That would be bad. But I would hope most people recognize how hard the police are working on this case and won't listen to his propaganda. He's not thinking clearly because he's been through so much."

Tate cradled her head as he pulled her into him, kissing her passionately as she felt herself fall deeper. "Do you know how much you are loved and wanted?"

"I want you to," she whispered as she pulled away just enough to kiss his neck. He moaned softly into her hair. She thought for a second about where Candy was in the house, but the thought fluttered right past her as Tate laid down on top of her on the sofa.

"Thank you for cooking dinner." Tate whispered in her ear before kissing her cheek. "You are so beautiful."

She giggled against his chest. "You're welcome for the dinner, but I think you're just trying to butter me up with that beautiful stuff."

Pulling himself up on his elbows so his piercing blue-gray eyes stared into her hazel ones, she could not deny the love and adoration showing through them. He touched her shoulder lightly with his fingers. "I am trying to butter you up, but you are beautiful, and I'm going to keep telling you that for the rest of our lives. So, you may as well get used to it. I can't wait to see you on our wedding day. I can't wait to have you step on my toes with your two left feet when we dance together..."

She snickered, kissing him again. "We can get

a pair of steel-toed boots for your toes... just in case."

He chuckled, placing his forehead against hers until their noses touched. "See, now you're thinking. Are you ready to go to bed?"

She raised her eyes to the ceiling, pretending to be thinking, before looking back at him and nodding. "Yeah. We should probably go into the bedroom before Candy walks in on something."

Pulling himself off the sofa first, Tate reached out a hand to help her up and walked her into their bedroom. As the bedroom door shut behind them, the worry about the backlash from Joshua Landry's words fell away, at least for the moment. If there was one thing being together did for them, it was put their worries in the back of their mind. Tate's eyes had a way of drawing her in and getting her lost.

Falling into bed with him and looking into his eyes, a flutter of excitement filled her chest, just as it always did when he was near her. Wrapping her arms around him, she tugged him into a passionate kiss while they sightlessly pulled at each other's clothing, trying to make sense of zippers and buttons that needed undoing. Their need to be together was like starvation, like they couldn't wait one second longer, and it was the best they had ever tasted.

Once they had their fill, curling into Tate's arms that night, breathless and tingling, worry about the case of murdered women found its way back into Hazel's mind. The person responsible was a predator, and he wouldn't stop until he was caught. Until then, there would always be a space in her mind reserved for them.

***

Using a tomb for cover, she watched as Tate faced down the barrel of a pistol. She knew this scene well. It was the moment before Harmony, the killer of her best friend and her best friend's boyfriend, pulled the trigger, shooting the man she loved. The terror she felt was palpable, but all she could do was watch the scene play out. Candy was there, too, just as she had been, standing sentinel between the aim of the two guns, debating how she could help Tate without a corporeal form.

She looked at Hazel, her eyes wide with a warning to stay hidden. Hazel gingerly moved further behind the massive stone structure, but not too far to see what was happening behind it. Tate pleaded with the unhinged young woman, but he did not seem to get through to her. Instead, Harmony began rambling and swinging her handgun wildly. Before Tate had more than a chance to flinch, the gun fired.

***

"PTSD is a bitch," Hazel grumbled as she poured her morning coffee. Candy sat playfully atop the kitchen table. Jake, also present in her kitchen that morning, sat in a chair as though he had a physical body.

"Tell me about it. Thankfully, I was preoccupied on the anniversary of my death day... with Jake's murder and stuff."

Candy's smile fell into a grimace before her impenetrable armor hid whatever emotions she was feeling. Jake reached over and placed a hand on her back as she flashed him a sad smile. Hazel sat in the chair next to Candy's legs and patted them. Even when she had her pajamas on in the morning, she had grown used to having Jake around. It was worth it to have a spectral companion for Candy. He was someone who could share with Candy what she could not.

"Love you," Hazel said, blowing Candy a kiss.

Candy smiled, before planting an icy kiss on Hazel's cheek. "Awe... I love you too. What's on your agenda for the day?"

"You mean besides housewife duties and getting over one nightmare to prepare for another?" Hazel mustered a frown, not because of the fact she was staying home but because her nightmares were relentless.

"We need to find you a hobby."

"Yeah... I could use one. Anyway, I'm going to at least get dressed. I'll be back." Rising from the table, Hazel walked to her bedroom, careful not to spill the cup of coffee in her hand.

As she dressed for the day, Tate texted her, letting her know Detective Bourgeois wanted to meet with her again.

I guess I'm not staying home today.

Her stomach became tense as her mind swirled around what the detective could have to talk to her about and the thought of it having something to do with Joshua Landry's escapade in the swamp. Deciding that heading to the police station right away was better than dwelling on the meeting all day, she grabbed her bag and made her way to her car.

Meeting with Detective Bourgeois for the second time was a bit easier on Hazel's nerves than the first. At least this time, she knew he believed in her abilities. After following Emily Landry's spirit to find Emily's husband in the swamp with a gun, there left little doubt for what she could do. Tate was already at work, so she knew he was somewhere in the building, unless he was out on a call. Either way, it made her feel better just knowing he was nearby. Sitting in the lobby, waiting for the detective to retrieve her, she realized she did not have any new information for him, so she hoped he had something new to share with her.

"Hazel." A man's voice sounded as Hazel stared at her hands in her lap. Detective Bourgeois stood over her with his hand extended. Reaching out to grab his hand, she lifted herself off the chair and did her best to calm her anxiety while following him to the office at the back of the building. The familiar feeling of being summoned to the principal's office flooded over her as soon as she got into the hall, so she began gnawing her fingernails as they made their way to his office.

The noise of the bustling precinct was drowned out as he closed the door behind her.

"Have a seat, Hazel... How are you feeling today? Mitchell told me about your fainting spell at the Landry's house." He sat at his desk, lowering his eyebrows as he waited for her response.

Her eyes cast downward as she felt her cheeks flush.

"I'm okay. I think I'll remember breakfast from now on."

She knew low blood sugar was not why she passed out, but she was not ready to divulge that fact to the detective. Her stories had been strange enough, even if they were real.

He smiled as he pulled a file out of his desk drawer.

"I'm assuming you saw the news last night?"

She nodded, knowing exactly what he was talking about. Emily Landry's husband decided to wage a public war on the police department, and Detective Bourgeois was visibly worried about the possible fallout.

"It's not often we deal with the loved one of a victim who takes the route Joshua Landry has decided to take. As I explained to him, it's only going to make the investigation into his wife's murder more difficult, but he was undeterred." The detective paused, fumbling with his ink pen cap. "I'm not sure what his plans are since getting released, but I'm hoping it doesn't involve any more guns in the swampland."

Hazel made a noncommittal sound in the back of her throat. She had no idea what Joshua had planned, although she was beginning to feel like the detective would want her to find out.

"Anyway... I called you here today for a few reasons. The first reason was to check in on you. I brought you to the Landry's house, but I hadn't spoken to you since you left. Although I spoke to Tate, and he assured me you were okay, I wanted to check in. The other reason I wanted to speak to you was to find out if you had spoken to Emily again... I was hoping there was more to uncover here... something more to help us to help her."

She pretended to think for a moment, but she knew there was no more useful information in her brain to share. She had already told the detective everything, aside from the vision during her fall.

"I wish I had more information... but I've already told you all I know. Emily was in her yard when I was there, but she didn't share any new information. She was worried about her husband. I haven't seen Malerie or Jessica Barrios since before the last time I met with you. I'm not sure why they've been scarce." She paused to consider a possibility she was almost too afraid to offer. "Last time I saw Jessica... the only time I saw her... was when we went to search the swamp for Michelle's body. Maybe if I returned there..."

Her eyebrows raised as she watched the lightbulb in his head turned on. "You think you'd see her?"

Hazel hesitated, but nodded slowly.

"Would you want to go there today? I can take you."

Dread flooded back to her, filling every available crevice. Going back to the swamp was not on her short list of things to do, or on her long list, for that matter. She knew she had to, but it did not make it any easier to stomach.

"Yes, but I admit to being sickened by the thought of returning there."

He frowned. "I understand it can't be easy. I know about what happened to you earlier in the summer, and I respect the hell out of you for your bravery."

She could not help but to chuckle slightly.

I'm anything but brave.

She looked at the floor, but felt his eyes on her.

"You know, Hazel, I hope I'm not out of line to suggest this... but I've had many officers develop post-traumatic stress disorder on this job... and if you feel you need help to cope with what happened to you, there are people out there who can try to help. I'm not trying to diagnose you, by any means, but just in case you believe this to be the case... I wanted to make sure you knew."

She knew he was right, but she did not know how to respond, so all she could do was nod. She did not enjoy talking about her emotional trauma to anyone, especially not a stranger. The room remained quiet for several minutes as she waited for him to save her from the effort of speaking first.

"Well, I'll just leave it at that. Do you want to

go back to the swamp? You don't have to do it if it makes you uncomfortable."

"No. I want to help. I'll be okay. I'd like Tate to come, though. If that's okay."

Detective Bourgeois nodded his head. "Absolutely. Do you want to text him, or should I?"

Hazel pulled her phone out of her bag, unlocking the screen and selecting the top contact. "I'll text him. Thank you."

Her anxiety rose as time clicked by until she felt nearly wound up enough to pop, but Tate's presence would help to calm her. Tate responded to her text quickly, to her relief. Thankfully, he was close to the precinct and said he would be there in a few minutes. She shared the update with Detective Bourgeois, who told her he had one errand to run so he would head out and meet her and Tate at the search location. She was relieved to ride there with only Tate in the car. Being alone with him would help her get control of her stress level before venturing back into the swamp. Returning to the lobby, she sat down to wait for Tate's arrival.

Heading to the swamp for the second time, she suddenly regretted her decision to wear sandals.

"You don't still have rain boots in your trunk, do you?"

Tate shot her a sideways glance before cracking a smile.

"Maybe... if you can manage them being too big for your feet."

"Ah..." She leaned over to glance at Tate's boots before looking back at her own nearly bare feet. "I guess I'll have to just waddle around in them then. I don't want to go home with a tick, or worse."

Tate nodded. "Yes... we wouldn't want that. Or I could just carry you."

She giggled and reached out to hold his hand. He took it happily.

By the time they pulled up to the lot where they needed to park, Detective Bourgeois was already parked and eating what looked to be a sandwich while leaning against his car.

"Hey y'all," the detective said as Hazel and Tate exited Tate's police cruiser. Detective Bourgeois was already wearing rain boots that went to his knees. Hazel went around to the back of Tate's vehicle and put on his rain boots, although they were several inches too big for her. It was still better than getting mud between her toes. Tate walked over to shake the detective's hand. Hazel stood back for a few minutes while the two men chatted, only walking over when Tate reached out a hand to her. Her nerves were still buzzing like there were bees in her stomach, but she actively worked to calm herself before venturing into the marsh. She hoped they would not happen upon the body of Michelle Barrilleaux. One happy ending after three murdered women seemed like asking for a miracle, but it was a hope she held onto.

Standing beside the two chatting men, Hazel thought she caught a glimmer of movement in her peripheral vision. She cleared her throat.

"I think I need to start walking," she said, interrupting their conversation. She did not even know what they were talking about, but it did not seem to matter. The pull on her was too strong to ignore. They both acknowledged her when she spoke, turning to face her direction.

"Okay, are you ready, detective?" Tate asked.

The detective nodded, and they all began walking towards the tree line.

Hazel no longer saw what she thought she had seen before, but she still walked in its direction, hoping it was one of the spirits she knew, and not a Louisiana swamp monster. She learned, through the many nightmares that plagued her, that there was more to the swamp than met the eye. Her heart felt sluggish as her limbs started to tingle. Something was summoning her, almost like she was a puppet on invisible strings, although she could not see the puppet master. She was glad to be in a heavily wooded area, and not an area that was all underwater. She would rather bring home a tick than an alligator bite or a leech, either of which was possible in the environment she was venturing into.

They walked only a couple of hundred yards into the tree line when she caught another glimpse of a spectral form near a cluster of trees. She tugged on Tate's hand and headed in its direction. From her distance, she could not yet tell whose spirit it was. Her heart pounded loud enough as she worried the spirit could be Michelle. Her heart wanted to believe there was still hope of finding the woman alive, but her mind argued that possibility with every step she took. They traversed the wet ground at a quick pace, crossing over large tree roots and areas of ankle-deep water. The spirit did not stand idly by and wait for them, but continued to glide deeper into the wetlands.

"Who do you see?" Detective Bourgeois asked, a slight panic showed on his voice.

"I don't know yet... she won't stay still." Hazel began to get flustered with the marathon she was being made to run. She did not understand why the spirit would not simply stay still and let her catch up. Hazel was clearly not meant for running races and her labored breaths were proof of that.

She could almost make out a flurry of chocolate hair, which would narrow down the spirit's identity to either Malerie or Emily, but she was not close enough to know for sure. "Wait for me, please!" she called out, but the woman continued to dart in the opposite direction. She wanted to stop to catch her breath, but she had already run too far to quit, too far to lose the spirit.

As they rounded another group of trees, the spirit was finally standing still, allowing Hazel to catch up with her. Bracing her hands on her knees, Hazel panted, trying to regulate her breathing. Her body was no longer running a marathon, but her heart was. Approaching the woman gingerly, Hazel held up her hand, silently telling the men to stay back. They obliged, staying where they were while she ventured forward.

Hazel swallowed back something bitter as she reached out to touch the spirit on the arm. "Emily."

Emily appeared paralyzed. Her blue eyes stared down at something unseen on the ground. She pointed a haunting hand at whatever caught her eye, but Hazel was not able to decipher an object out of the tangle of mud and weeds. She hesitated, almost too scared to find whatever was buried in the ground. Squatting to get a closer look, she reached down and began passing her hand over the long grass, hoping something would reveal itself that was not a venomous snake.

A hint of metal gleamed in the meager

sunlight shining through the trees. Looking up to meet the spirit's eyes for confirmation, Emily's face remained etched with determination. She nodded solemnly. Hazel's stomach wove into a knot as she waved the officers over to her side. They approached her immediately. Detective Bourgeois pulled on a pair of latex gloves as he walked. Moving out of the way, Tate and the detective took her place, searching among the weeds.

Taking a similar sentinel stance next to Emily, Hazel was unable to look away as the officers hovered over the muddy ground, but unsure what they would find or what it would mean. When Detective Bourgeois raised the metal object to drop it into a small plastic bag, Hazel felt slightly underwhelmed. After all the running through the marsh and cryptic body language, all they found was a silver key. There were countless doors that key could open. Hazel looked at Emily to ask her what the key belonged to, but the spirit was already gone.

14

Signs

Tate and Detective Bourgeois did a thorough search of the surrounding marsh before calling in the forensic team to look at the area further. Emily did not reappear, so after hours within the dreaded swamp, the trio made the long and arduous march back to the parking lot. The detective met the rest of the team in order to brief them on his intended search, but Hazel and Tate climbed back into his car for the long drive home.

The drive back to their side of the city was

slow as rush hour traffic was just beginning, although the time of the day in New Orleans made little a difference. Having to stop back in the downtown area to get Hazel's car only made it a longer drive. She could not stop wondering why Emily had not spoken to her in the swamp. She had only stood there. Spirits could be so cryptic sometimes and it was not at all helpful. This was the one time when Hazel hoped to see a spirit in her rear-view mirror or in her sleep, anywhere in which she could get more information about what she needed to know to help solve the case. It had been weighing her down for long enough and the victim count kept growing.

Tate stopped to grab dinner for them, so Hazel got home before he did and jumped into the shower immediately to clean the marsh off her. She was about to dip her head under the stream of water when a familiar mane of red hair popped through the shower door.

"You reek!" Candy grimaced, eyeing Hazel's mud-streaked legs.

"Duh. That's why I'm taking a shower. A bit

202 C. A. Varian

of privacy would be good, though, unless there was a point to this visit."

Candy pulled her head out of the shower, but still peered through the glass. This was an intrusion Hazel had grown used to. "Not really, just missed you. Jake phased out hours ago. How did it go with the detective?"

"It was my bright idea to go back to where Jessica Barrios' body was found, so I guess I made the day harder on myself."

Hazel had meant the comment to be sarcastic, but the heaviness in her body told a different story. She did not think she was fooling Candy, either.

She could see Candy slowly shake her head before responding. "I should have gone with you today. I don't like you putting yourself into situations that will make your nightmares worse."

"Tate came with me. Plus, you had Jake here. It was not a problem. I'm okay."

Even if she would have felt better having Candy there, she did not want Candy to feel guilty about doing something for herself. Hazel still fought with guilt because she depended on

Candy too much, and that she may be the reason Candy never crossed over, so she did not want Candy to sacrifice time with Jake to watch over her when she did not need to. She had done enough of that in the past year.

Once Tate returned from picking up their dinner, the two of them ate and then cuddled on the sofa while watching a romantic comedy. Her experiences from the day filled her mind, but she tried to push them away as she cuddled with Tate. His touch made it hard to think about anything else, but his touch wasn't able to protect her as she slept. Those visions were uninhibited, free to traumatize her fragile mind.

***

Pulling in ragged breaths, she stumbled through the marsh, tripping on a tree root, and tumbling to the ground. Loud steps sounded behind her. Too close. They were too close. She clawed at the earth, pulling herself back onto shaky legs and rushing ahead. She ran with no destination in mind. Her mind unable to focus on anything but escape. Her daughter was still in the playhouse in their yard. She had to keep him away from Bella, no matter what. The compulsion to

---

look back flooded her senses, but it would only slow her down. The footsteps were sign enough of how close he was. Or was it the sound of her heartbeat thrashing in her ears? She could not be sure. Either way, the beats led her farther from home.

***

Crying herself awake, Hazel was drenched with sweat. She grasped the sides of her head and squeezed, as she bolted upright, trying to close the door that allowed spirits to invade her mind and fill it with traumatizing images. She thought she wanted to see Emily again, so she could understand more about her murder, but she changed her mind. Instead, she wanted it to all go away. Living a different, disturbing life in her dreams every night was too much. She could not take it anymore.

"Baby... are you okay?" Tate reached over to touch her arm. She had not even realized he was still in the bed.

Trying to calm her face, she turned to assure him she was fine, but her face crumpled. Instead of responding, she laid back down, curling up into the crook of his arm. Her ears rang, and she was overcome with the need for comfort.

Instead of pressing her for a response, Tate passed his fingers gently across her back. Even with the emptiness that had developed in her stomach, electricity still found a way to pass through her with each touch.

"It's going to be okay, you know," he said as he kissed the top of her head. "I know it doesn't seem that way when you wake up from these nightmares... but they aren't your life in there. And for that, you should be grateful."

He paused, pulling away just enough to look into her eyes. She fought the urge to avoid eye contact. It had always been her instinct to do so. But she could not do that with Tate. So, after a struggle within herself, she lifted tear-stained eyes to meet his. He smiled, wiping her cheek with his thumb.

"I don't want to be a burden..." She closed her eyes as the heaviness in her stomach increased with her admission. "Every time I witness one of these experiences, it makes me feel damaged... like it breaks off a piece of me. You deserve someone who is whole."

206 C. A. Varian

Emotion flashed through his eyes as he pulled her back into him. "You have been telling me stuff like that since I first kissed you, and I'm still here. I'm not sure what it will take for you to realize that you are enough, more than enough. I hate how these visions make you feel, and how I wish I had a way to take that away from you. But those visions do not make you any less of a woman. If anything, they make you more special. You can do something most other people cannot do. And I know those abilities often come as a burden, but you are so strong." He pulled her face to his and kissed her deeply. Salt tasted on her lips as his tears mixed with hers. Her heart broke. She had hurt him again, even if he did not admit it.

"Tate... I... I'm sorry."

He kissed her again, harder this time. "Don't apologize to me. Okay? You have no reason to apologize to me. I am sorry that I can't take this burden away from you, but you have nothing to apologize for. You were born this way, and I love you the way you are."

Hazel nodded into his chest, allowing herself to absorb his words. The message may not make it into the deepest corners of her being, but at least it could get her through the morning.

"Thank you."

He squeezed her shoulders gently, filling her with warmth. "You're welcome. What do you have on the agenda today?"

She shrugged. "I'm not sure. I'll have to talk to Candy. I'd like to spend some time with her. Maybe she and I can put our heads together and cook something for dinner."

"Hey... the pasta the two of y'all made was great. I'm not sure what we have for ingredients, but the market isn't too far."

"Thanks. It wasn't too difficult. I may get the hang of cooking after all. Any requests for tonight?"

She felt him smile against the top of her head.

"As long as you're my dinner date, I don't care."

When Tate left for work, Hazel felt a renewed sense of purpose. She felt a little better about the vivid nightmares she suffered at night, because she knew he was right about the importance of her abilities. She also knew she had to get it through her head that he was there for the long haul. It was simply hard to change a mentality she had carried for her entire life. Self-doubt had always plagued her, but she had come a long way in the past year, and she needed to accept that. Forcing a deep breath into her nose, and then out of her mouth, she climbed out of her bed and left her bedroom in search of Candy.

Not seeing her best friend in any of the main rooms of the house, she knocked lightly on Candy's bedroom door. Instead of answering, Candy apparently thought it more effective to stick her head through the door like Nearly Headless Nick had done with the table in the first Harry Potter movie, and it had a similar effect as Hazel jumped back, nearly peeing on herself.

"Geez, Candy! Why are you always poking your head through things and scaring me?"

Candy laughed as Hazel opened the bedroom door with one hand still glued to her chest.

"Because it works every time, doll."

Flopping onto the bed next to Candy, Hazel sighed loudly. "You're going to give me a heart attack." She hesitated, unsure if she wanted to open the assortment of problems circling through her mind. Just the thought of it made her uneasy. "I was thinking about going back to Celeste... the elderly woman who I met with when I was working on Angela's case. She practices Wicca."

Candy lifted herself up onto her elbows, eyes gleaming with excitement. "Ooh. For what? I thought that kind of stuff freaked you out."

Hazel cringed at the reminder. "It does, but I was hoping she could help me with my dreams... or maybe help me unlock more of them. Most of the time, I feel like I'm seeing events I cannot change and that I can't pull anything helpful out of them. If I'm going to suffer through them, I want to be able to do more. If that's at all possible."

Candy considered this, nodding quickly. "I think it's a great idea. Can I come with you?"

"Let's see..." Hazel pursed her lips, scratching her chin thoughtfully. Candy gasped. "I suppose, but don't make me look crazy. After the questions I asked her last time, she probably already thinks I'm nuts."

"I'm 100% positive she already thinks you're crazy... just saying. But I will refrain from being too much of a distraction."

"Uh... thanks. I think. I'm going to call her and see if she can meet with me. She was really knowledgeable about the stone in Angela's sapphire necklace when I met with her last time. If she knows even half that much about dreams, maybe she can help me... well, if she knows about my particular brand of dreams."

Pulling her cellphone out of her pocket, she searched for Celeste's contact information and dialed her number. The call only rang once before Celeste's voice greeted her.

"Hazel, dear, so good of you to call me."

She was not expecting Celeste to recognize her phone number after such a long time of not speaking and having only met once. She bit her lip, still debating what to say.

"Thank you for taking my call, Miss Celeste."

"Are you calling about another stone? I'd love to have you over for tea again and we could discuss it."

The knot living somewhere in Hazel's chest loosened.

"I did want to talk to you about something, but not about a stone. I wondered how much you knew about dreams?"

"If you want to know about dreams, my dear, then you've called the right lady. Will you be coming by today?"

Hazel glanced over to Candy, who was nodding her head vigorously, and then told Miss Celeste that she would be on her way before hanging up the call and flopping back onto the bed.

"This ought to be interesting." Candy jumped off the bed, twirling her abnormally long red locks around her finger.

"Yeah. I would be lying if I said I wasn't nervous."

***

After some quick grooming and dressing, Hazel and Candy piled into her sedan and headed south in the direction of Celeste's cottage. She drove with one hand on the wheel, and the other fingers ended up inside of her mouth so she could gnaw feverishly on her nails. It was a disgusting habit. She knew that, but it was not one she was going to solve that day. Celeste had always been kind to her, so part of her knew she was probably overreacting. The other part of her battled the desire to flee as she pasted on a smile and put her car into park.

The first time she had driven to Celeste's small cottage on the outskirts of the city, she remembered thinking how at home fairies would be living among the wildflowers, if only the Louisiana mosquitos were not big enough to eat them. The thought made her chuckle. Candy, curled up in the seat beside her, stared out of the window with wanderlust blooming across her face.

"This place is magical," Candy said. Her blue eyes were bright as she scanned the property.

The house still looked charming, with its wind chimes and birdhouses. The small garden was well maintained, although Celeste had to be in her seventies, and there were little wooden sculptures carefully placed throughout the landscaped yard. Unlike many of the properties within the city that sported mostly roses or azaleas, this yard was filled with mostly wildflowers that were scattered throughout the yard as though their seeds took flight and sprouted where they landed.

Floating out of the car, Candy explored the

yard, peaking into the birdhouses and carefully handling the flower blooms to smell them. A smile crept across Hazel's face while she watched Candy, who was childlike while exploring the property. Before getting out of the car, Hazel sent a quick text message to Tate, assuring him she had gotten there safe and promising to let him know when she was on her way home.

Wiping sweaty palms against legs of her jeans, she opened her car door and plodded to the front porch. Although the temperature outside was feeling more like Fall, the humidity was still thick enough to cut with a knife. She pulled a thick breath into her nose and blew it slowly out of her mouth as she approached the familiar purple front door. Candy, noticing Hazel's ascent up the porch, abandoned her adventure through the yard and accompanied Hazel to the front door.

Although she had been nervous all morning, Celeste's wide smile was disarming. Her long blond hair had been pulled back into a low ponytail and her bright blue eyes sparkled when she smiled. Just as she had the first time Hazel met her, Celeste wore more layers of clothes than could be comfortable in the South Louisiana heat. Her long Bohemian style skirt was made from various patches of brightly colored fabric, and she had on a white blouse layered over by a lace vest. Hazel appreciated the style, although she knew she could never pull it off herself.

"Welcome back, dear. So good to see you again!"

Celeste opened the door wide enough to allow Hazel to cross the threshold. With brief hesitation, she checked to see that Candy was behind her before entering the woman's home.

"Thank you for agreeing to see me again. I hope it wasn't too much of an inconvenience."

Celeste waved her hand nonchalantly. "Nonsense, dear. I'm glad for the company. Now, how about you go wait in my tearoom and I'll get the kettle."

Already knowing where the tearoom was, Hazel nodded briefly and made her way to the back of the house. The small room towards the back of the house still held a plethora of Wiccan artifacts, however Hazel was not as drawn to examine them since she had seen them before. Candy, on the other hand, still felt a sense of adventure and began making her way around the perimeter of the room, poking and prodding everything she could get her hands on. She rambled as she scanned the strange items, but Hazel's attention was drawn to the tune Celeste was singing. The old woman's voice carried across the house as though she intentionally wanted Hazel to hear her.

The lyrics, unmistakably from the Cajun French language, were unknown to Hazel, but the song flowed beautifully out of the old woman's mouth and into Hazel's ears. She only recognized two words, cher and gris-gris. She knew the word cher from hearing it around the city. It was pronounced as sha and meant dear or darling. Cajun people typically used it as a pet name. Gris-gris meant to put a spell on someone. Living in the heart of New Orleans, where faiths such as Voodoo and other pagan traditions were well known, everyone knew what gris-gris meant.

Before she could think about any more of the lyrics, Celeste entered the doorway, a silver tray balanced precariously in her hands. Hazel stood up and helped the tray onto the small table between their two chairs before taking her seat again.

Celeste's hands shook slightly as she held her teacup to her lips. Hazel reached out for her own, blowing on the steaming liquid to cool it.

"Well, what brings you to see me today, dear. I'm under no illusion you came here just to visit."

A flush swept across Hazel's cheeks at Celeste's words. She did not know how to approach her reason for being there. She bit her lip.

"I'm not even sure if you can help me, but I was so impressed by your knowledge of things... well, other worldly... last time I met with you, I thought you may be able to."

Celeste nodded as she smiled kindly, although she did not interrupt. Hazel recognized she was allowing her the time to explain what her needs were, so she continued.

"I'm curious what you know about dreams... but not just regular dreams. My dreams are more complicated."

Hazel watched the old woman's blue eyes as they almost appeared to flick up in Candy's direction before returning to look at her. She pretended not to notice.

"Are your dreams related to the spirit world, by chance? Is that what makes them complicated?"

Hazel's mouth opened and closed a few times before she consciously forced it to stop. She felt a mixture of validation and a loss for words. She glanced at Candy, who nodded in encouragement. Looking back at Celeste, she nodded hesitantly.

Celeste set down her teacup, leaning forward to take Hazel by the hands. Fighting her usual instinct to pull away, she allowed the woman to hold her hands, shifting slightly in her chair as chills ran through her body. Candy, sensing Hazel's uneasiness, moved in closer. Celeste closed her eyes and hummed quietly. The song made the hair on the back of Hazel's neck stand up.

When Celeste's eyes reopened, they held a knowing that made Hazel uncomfortable. It was almost like she had looked inside of Hazel's mind and knew everything Hazel had witnessed in her own mind.

"For most people," Celeste began, "dreaming gives them the opportunity to work through things in their unconscious mind that they could not work out in their conscious mind. You are less inhibited in your dreams, and can therefore look at things without the limitations you face in life. For you, however, dreams give you the opportunity to plunge into lives of others, with the freedom of a bird scanning the sky for prey. I can feel from your aura that you don't trust enough in your abilities to use the freedoms dreams allow you, so you can take control of your senses. But you must learn how to control your dreams so you can seek the wisdom they are trying to show you. You are missing signs, Hazel, dreadfully important ones."

Hazel swallowed thickly, overwhelmed by what Celeste was saying to her, unsure how to respond. Celeste continued.

"Those who share their dreams with you are doing it with a purpose. There is something they want you to see. Maybe it's a person, or a place, but it's important."

She swallowed thickly, feeling flustered. "But it's so hard to focus on the important symbols in my dreams when I'm literally running for my life." A sob left Hazel as the horror of her nightmares flooded into her mind. Dreams of being tied up, running from a murderer, stored in the trunk of a car heading to her death all plagued her. She hated them. She did not want to treat them like a treasure hunt. Candy began petting her head as tears burned the back of her eyes, but Hazel shook her off. She did not want to calm down; she wanted it to stop.

Celeste nodded. Her eyes were filled with sympathy. "I understand it must be hard, child. Most people could not handle a gift such as yours. I do not have the ability to prevent these dreams from flooding your mind when you sleep. I can do some simple spells to try to protect you as you venture into these dangerous circumstances. I also want you to keep a journal as soon as you wake every morning. Try to keep a list of things that stand out to you in these dreams. You may find what you're looking for."

"What does she mean by a spell?" asked Candy, leveling her face with Hazel's. "Like an actual spell?"

Hazel shrugged. She did not have any answers.

Her limbs felt heavy and her body felt drained of all energy. She stared at the ground as Celeste shuffled around the room, digging through cabinets and drawers, dropping random items into a small wicker basket. The shuffling feet stopped only a few inches from Hazel's own shoes, causing Hazel to look up at the elderly woman staring down at her. Hazel flinched as a pair of sharp scissors came at the back of her neck.

15

Protection Spell

Hazel was too slow to stop the descent of the scissors as they snipped a lock of hair off the back of her head.

"What in the hell?" She reached back to where her hair had been cut, her face falling into a genuine scowl.

"Yeah! What in the hell?" Candy's reaction was more delayed than Hazel's had been. Hazel shot a sideways glance at her before looking back at Celeste, who returned to her seat.

"Calm down, dear. I needed a lock of your hair for the protection spell. You really are jumpy." Celeste's voice was soft, but Hazel felt like she was being facetious.

"You could have told me before you chopped my hair off." Hazel crossed her arms around her chest as she frowned. She watched as Celeste carved the word protection on one side of the tall white candle and her name on the other side, before wrapping the brunette lock around it. A new scent wafted across the room, although Hazel could not make out what it was.

"What's that smell?" She fumbled through the ingredients on the table, looking for the bottle of fragrance.

"Amber. It's needed for the protection spell to work."

Placing the candle into an intricate holder, Celeste leaned over and lit it before taking Hazel's hands once again.

"You will burn this protection candle for ten minutes every day until it goes out. It's meant to protect you from harm, but that doesn't mean you should throw yourself into dangerous situations just to test its power."

Skeptical, but desperate for any help Celeste could give, Hazel nodded her head before closing her eyes while the candle burned.

The warm, powdery, sweet scent drifted throughout the room, crawling its way into Hazel's nostrils as she focused her mind on it protecting her.

Arriving home later that afternoon, she set the protection candle in a candleholder in her bedroom. She did not know if it made any difference in her safety, but it was easy enough to burn it and hope it did. She filled Tate in on her day while they lay in bed that night. Although he was also skeptical about the effectiveness of any spell, he appreciated Celeste's advice for Hazel to not depend on the protection spell and to practice common sense. If she was to take anything away from their meeting, it was for her to make better decisions about how she proceeded in murder investigations. Not that she was known for good decision making.

***

Holding her breath as her back leaned against the door, she listened as the floorboards on the deck creaked beneath the creature's feet. Her chest was squeezed into a vise as her lungs starved for oxygen, but she couldn't make a sound. She begged for her mind to make sense of what she had seen. Her eyes saw a seven-foot-tall swamp monster, but her mind told her it had to have been something else. Swamp monsters did not exist. It couldn't be.

Silent tears dripped down her cheek, landing gently on the floor as she held her ear to the door, hoping the creature would leave. Gentle scrapes sounded on the door, just loud enough to hear. It was toying with her. It knew she was inside. Scrapes turned into light taps. Her eyes desperately scanned the room for a weapon. Knives in the kitchen were her only hope, but it would hear her if she walked across the room. She was too scared to move. Her cellphone was in her pocket, but she already knew she would not be able to use it. With the heavy trees of the marshland and the state line being so close, cellular signal was almost nonexistent. That was why she visited her parents' fishing camp during her time off work. She wanted the seclusion so she could unwind, fish, and catch up on her reading. But she never expected this to happen.

Light knocking turned into banging. The door

vibrated against her back as the creature scrabbled to get inside. She had to get a weapon. She had to risk it.

Wiping the tears from her cheek, she set her face before tiptoeing to the kitchen and grasping a butcher knife. Debating where the safest place in the cabin would be, she ran into the bathroom and quietly locked the door. She clinched her teeth as she fumbled with the lock on the window, hoping she was small enough to fit through it if she needed to make a quick escape. Just as she inched the window up, she heard a crash as the front door slammed open.

***

"I want to go back to my old apartment... just to see if she's there. I haven't seen Malerie face to face since that time she approached me in the parking lot. Actually, that's the only place I've ever seen her besides in my dreams. I don't know why she hasn't followed me here... I can't believe I'm even complaining about this."

"Neither can I," said Candy, eyeing Hazel like she may have lost her mind. "Be careful what you wish for. You don't want all three of them to start showing up at the foot of your bed every night."

Hazel rolled her eyes, returning her attention

226 C. A. Varian

to the coffeemaker. "I know. I have my hands full enough with you doing that."

"Oh, come on! You know you like it when I try to time it just right to pop up on top of lover boy."

Hazel turned around to swat at Candy, only to miss, as she always did. Candy disappeared, re-manifesting her form across the kitchen.

"You'd better watch out or I'm going to tell your lover boy."

Candy pulled her hand in front of her face and mouthed a dramatic "Oh no!" before blowing Hazel a kiss and hopping onto the kitchen table, swinging her legs playfully from side to side.

"I can't tell you how much I enjoy these little chats of ours." Hazel poured her coffee and sat in the chair next to Candy, as she did every morning.

"You know I love you, doll." Candy's smile gleamed. Hazel forced a scowl in return. "Ooh! We should go look at wedding dresses!"

Hazel cringed internally at the thought of wearing a wedding dress. With everything that had been going on, she hadn't given her and Tate's wedding a lot of thought. It almost felt wrong to plan a wedding when three women had just been murdered and one was still missing. It would be different if those women were not relying on her to solve the crime for them. But, under the circumstances, feeling joyful felt like cheating them somehow.

"Do I really have to wear one? I mean... it's not exactly my style."

Candy burst into a fit of laughter, slapping absently at the air in front of her, before dramatically pretending to have a hard time stopping herself. "Hazel... doll... you have no style. Ugh, you kill me sometimes!"

Staring at Candy open mouthed, Hazel tried to plan her response but knew Candy was right. It did not stop her from pretending to be mad, however. Their relationship was nothing if not middle grade leveled maturity.

"You are so mean today."

"Who's mean?" Tate asked as he came into the kitchen.

"Oh, good morning," Hazel said as she crossed the kitchen to kiss him. "Candy is mean. I said today, but she's mean like eighty percent of the time."

Candy gasped loudly, but Tate could not hear her. He chuckled as he walked to the coffeemaker. "Candy... don't be mean to my girl."

Even though Tate could not see or hear Candy, he still liked to talk to her and make sure she felt included in their life, which warmed Hazel's heart. She stuck her tongue out at Candy, who, in turn, flipped her off before disappearing.

"I think she went to her bedroom," Hazel said as she sat back down at the table. "She deserved to be punished, anyway. We should figure out a way to lock her ass in there when she's bad."

Abandoning his coffee on the table, Tate swooped down and gave her another kiss before sliding into the chair next to her. "That would be a dangerous power... but it would be helpful when you're trying to sleep."

"It certainly would. Are you about to head to work?"

Tate nodded, sipping his coffee. "But I'm off tomorrow and I can't wait to spend it with you. Anything special you'd like to do?"

"Honestly... I'd like to just stay home. I feel

like we haven't spent much time here, together, since I moved in. It would be good to do that. We could play games, or watch movies... whatever you'd like to do. I'd just like to do something at home."

A smile crawled across Tate's handsome face as he leaned over to kiss her. "I'm sure we will figure something out." Standing up from the table, Tate placed his mug in the sink and walked towards the door. "Well... I love you and I'll see you this afternoon."

"Love you, too!" Hazel called out after him as he left.

A call from Detective Bourgeois caught Hazel by surprise. He always communicated with her through Tate, at least when setting up meetings, so she was not even aware he had her phone number. Wanting to meet with her later that day, she opted to invite Candy along this time. Candy had been upset last time she met with him and ended up in the swamp, so she did not want a repeat of that experience.

When they arrived at the police station after lunch, Candy's usually free-spirited posture was replaced by something more rigid. She did not know if it was because she expected a return to the swamp, or if it was just being inside of a police station that had her on edge, but she did not dare ask her. She was already concerned about people within the department, thinking she was crazy with her claim to speak to spirits, so she did not want to be caught talking to the seemingly empty chair next to her.

Candy's tight-lipped mouth lifted into more of a smile when the handsome Detective Bourgeois approached them from the hall where his office was located. Hazel was not surprised but was glad to see a flicker of her friend's personality break through the stressful situation. As they followed the detective to his office, she watched Candy's eyes for just a moniker of entertainment, stifling her giggles as Candy's animated responses lit up her face. She wanted to remind Candy that the detective was happily married, and she was also happy in a relationship with Jake, but it was not like she could be with the detective anyway, so what was the harm?

Candy calmed her reactions as the detective closed the office door, realizing the conversation would be serious enough that she did not want to distract Hazel or make her seem insensitive by laughing, which Hazel quietly appreciated.

"How are you doing today, Hazel? I hope you don't mind me contacting you directly, but I figured I wouldn't keep bothering Tate while he's on patrol."

"Not at all, and I'm doing pretty good today."

"That's good to hear. So, I called you in because we had some updates from the lab and the search that I wanted to share with you. First of all, researchers combed the location where we found the key but found no other evidence. Recent rains unfortunately washed away any footprints that the owner of the key could have left behind. We still don't know what the key was for, or who it belonged to. There was a partial print on the key, but the environment it was found it damaged the print too much to compare it in the system."

"That sucks," Candy said. Hazel nodded as her heart felt like it shrank a little. She had been hoping the key would crack the case, at least a little, but it felt like the entire search had been for nothing.

"That's really unfortunate," she sighed. "I was hoping we didn't go through all that for nothing."

"We didn't do it all for nothing, Hazel. That area had not been pinned as part of the crime scene. Now it is. Jessica's body was found in a completely different part of the swamp. Also, I wanted to update you on Joshua's friend, Hunter Billiot. He's been released from jail as of yesterday."

"Who found her?" Candy asked. "Has that been made public?"

Hazel pondered this before sharing Candy's question with the detective. She had not even told Detective Bourgeois about Candy being there. It occurred to her she did not know who had found any of the women, or that it was even relevant, but maybe Candy was onto something. Hazel bit her lip, turning back to face the detective.

"Who found Jessica's body? Was it an officer or her family or...?"

He shuffled through folders on his desk, pulling out one with Jessica's name on it.

Opening it, he thumbed through until he found the paper he was looking for.

"Jessica was found by a group of five fishermen from Aberdeen Trucking Company. I believe they were on a company fishing trip or something."

A chill flooded Hazel's body at the mention of Aberdeen Trucking Company. When she was looking into the murder of Angela Spencer only months prior, the spirit had led her to a stack of evidence that included bank statements from Waters' Financial Firm. One of the entries that popped up repeatedly on those statements as having received deposits from the financial firm was Aberdeen Trucking Company. Raymond Waters had ended up being Angela's killer and had abducted Hazel, intending for her to become his fifth victim. She had barely escaped with her life. Visions of that bank statement haunted Hazel's dreams. But she had assumed they were side effects of the post-traumatic stress disorder she developed after the attack, and not relevant to the new case.

Detective Bourgeois noticed the change in her posture. He moved his chair closer to her, leaning his elbows onto his knees so he could look into her now lowered eyes.

"Hazel... does that name ring a bell for you?"

She hesitated, but ended up explaining the entire series of events to him. He did not interrupt her. Instead, his eyes seemed to double as she made the connections the police department had seemed to miss when investigating Raymond Waters' case. She did not know if Mr. Aberdeen had anything to do with the murders, but the coincidence was too big to ignore. The detective seemed to agree.

He took notes feverishly while she explained, nodding his head every few moments in acknowledgement. When she was finished speaking, he pulled his keyboard away from his computer and began typing. She could not see what he was looking for, but she remained quiet while he worked. After a few minutes of intense typing, he printed a sheet of paper and turned his eyes back to her.

"There's only so many ways we can play this, Hazel. So, I guess what I'm asking you is are you making an anonymous tip accusing Mr. Aberdeen of wrongdoing?"

"Uh..." She swallowed as she ran her fingers through her hair, getting caught in a tangle and grimacing as she pulled it out. "I don't follow."

He cleared his throat. "We can't just search his house without a warrant, but with enough of a reason, we can set up surveillance. So... what I'm asking is... do we have enough to watch Mr. Aberdeen based on what you believe to be true."

A warm flush passed over Hazel as her heart began to race. Could she send the police after this man on a hunch? "How tall is he?"

The detective's eyebrows lifted before he nodded gingerly and turned to his computer, realizing what she was getting at. He began typing again and scanning the screen. Once he found what he was looking for, he leaned back in his chair, as though he had found it.

"He's a tall guy... six foot five inches. Since he's been arrested before, for a domestic disturbance, we have his height on record."

"Domestic disturbance?" A steady strum of Hazel's heartbeat within her head. Had they found their man?

"His wife called the police on him when they got into a fight, and he punched a hole in the wall. He was booked, but made bail the same day. His wife ended up dropping the charges."

Hazel nodded as she bit her already short nails. "So, you can just watch him and see if anything turns up?"

"Yes. We can't go inside of his house or anything, but we can see if he makes any moves that would allow us to get a warrant."

"Okay. Yes. I think that would be the best plan for now."

Looking up to Candy, Hazel said, "go to the old apartment and look for Malerie. See what you can find out from her." Candy nodded before vanishing .

Detective Bourgeois tapped his pen on the desk before turning back to his computer. He didn't even flinch when she spoke to Candy, like he already figured she was there."Okay. I will get everything set up and will call you with an update. Thank you for coming in. Oh... and Hazel... be safe out there."

Lifting herself off the chair and making her way to exit the room, Hazel could barely fight against the pounding of her heart. Her vision swam in a sea of colors before it went black.

16

Invasion of
the Mind

A gun clicked as it was loaded. Joshua Landry sat at his kitchen table with a shotgun leaning against the wall. He laced his boots before checking the messages on his phone.

***

"Hazel... Hazel... are you okay? Wake up, Hazel."

***

A knock sounded at the door. Joshua grunted before standing from the table and answering it.

***

"Hazel! Come back to me. Someone call 911! Someone call Officer Cormier!"

***

Dressed in full camouflage, Hunter Billiot waited outside the door. An assault rifle stood in his hands.

***

The shaking of her shoulders pulled Hazel out of what seemed like a virtual reality dream. She was there, watching Joshua and Hunter with their guns in hand. Squinting against the light in the room, Hazel tried to open her eyes. Detective Bourgeois hovered over her. His eyes were wild as he tried to wake her. Another figure stood there, however. They were not alone, but she couldn't make out the face.

"Who's that?" she muttered, catching the

WHISPERS FROM THE SWAMP 239

detective by surprise. He turned his head to look for what had caught her eye, but he only turned back, slack jawed.

"There's no one else here, Hazel. I called for help, but no one is here yet."

The figure moved as she blinked rapidly until the spirit of Emily Landry came into focus.

Hazel's body tensed as she glared at the figure. "Did you do this to me? Attacked me?"

Emily's watery eyes stared at her apologetically. "I didn't mean to attack you, but you have to stop him! Please!"

Detective Bourgeois looked from her to behind himself, his mouth hanging open in confusion.

Loud footsteps hammered down the hall, causing Emily to fade from sight. Tate ran into the doorway, passing right through the vanishing spirit. Dropping to his knees next to her, he leaned over and began checking her for injuries.

"What happen? Hazel, are you okay? Did y'all call the ambulance?"

His voice was frantic as he leaned over her. His

tears made his eyes shine. Hazel, still a bit dazed, tried to sit up, but Tate forced her back down.

"Not yet, baby. You might have a concussion. Did you fall?"

She blinked as the swimming in her head began to recede.

"I think so. I was about to leave and then... Emily did this!"

Tate's features pulled tight as he scanned the room. "Emily forced this on you while you were awake again?" His tone came out as barely repressed anger.

The sound of footsteps and squeaking wheels got closer until two paramedics stood in the doorway. Panic set in as they started getting the stretcher ready for her.

"No. Tate, I'm okay. We have to go after Joshua."

He shook his head as his eyes widened.

"Hazel... no. You're hurt and I'm putting my foot down. You come first, not Joshua or Emily, or any spirit for that matter."

Her chest tightened as she shook her head vehemently.

"Hazel," said Detective Bourgeois. "Did you say it's something with Joshua?"

She had almost forgotten the detective was still in the room. She turned to face him. "Yes. He has a gun, and he's planning something. Him and his friend. You have to stop him."

With one nod, the detective grabbed his stuff off his desk and bolted out of the door. The paramedics stood off to the side, aware she didn't want to go with them.

Arching an eyebrow and placing his hand on her cheek, Tate sighed. "At least let them look you over," he said. "Then we can go to the Landry's house."

Holding the hand that lay on her cheek, she smiled. "Thank you."

The female paramedic moved in closer and proceeded to check her vitals and her head for injury. Thankfully, she had not hit her head on her fall, so she was unharmed from the incident. She and Tate headed out of the building once her exam was complete.

As they crossed the bridge over Lake Ponchartrain, Emily appeared in the back seat of Tate's car. Hazel wanted to scream at her after

242   C. A. Varian

what happened in the precinct, to tell her to go away and never return, but she could not do it. What Emily had done was an assault in every sense of the word, but Hazel understood why she did it, so she had to let it go.

Emily remained quiet as they drove, fading out after a few minutes. By the time they arrived at Joshua Landry's property, Detective Bourgeois was already parked in the driveway along with one other police car. Not seeing anyone outside, Hazel assumed they were in the house or in the swamp, but she hoped not the latter. Before getting out of the car, Tate made a call to the detective but received no answer. Hazel's stomach fell. Maybe they were too late. Maybe Joshua was out for police blood.

"Stay in the car. I'm going to check the house."

Before Hazel could respond, Tate climbed out of the car with his hand on his holster. Her legs felt like they had gone numb. She rubbed her hands across them to bring them back to life as she kept her eyes peeled on Tate's back. Going around to the front of the house first, Tate knocked on the door and waited for a few agonizing minutes, but no one answered. He then went to the back of the house, looking through a few windows as he passed. His face had become tense as he approached the back door, although she didn't expect anyone to answer. Just as he was making his way back to the car, Emily appeared just at the water's edge. The lead within Hazel's belly grew heavier. They were in the swamp. She had no doubt. Tate opened the car door, pulling her attention away from the water's edge.

"No one is inside, or at least they aren't answering," he said as he closed the door behind him. "I'm going to have to go in after them."

She clenched her jaw as visions of Tate being in the line of fire again flooded her mind. He had only just recovered from a gunshot wound to the shoulder. Harmony had come so close to taking him from her in the cemetery that day. Her chest hurt.

"Tate, no. It's too dangerous."

He passed his fingers through his hair as he shifted in his seat. When he turned to face her, she knew she was not going to win this discussion. He reached out and grabbed her

244 C. A. Varian

hand, lacing his fingers through hers. She found it difficult to meet his eye.

"Sweetie... I know you're scared, but it's my job. They're sending backup, but I have to go in after them."

Tears battled against her need to keep her composure.

"Emily is by the canal. At least let me talk to her first. Maybe we can find out what's going on. The swamp is so big... you may not find them otherwise. We don't know where they went or how many people are even in there."

"I don't want her to make you pass out again." The muscles in his face were taut as he looked deep into her eyes, although she kept looking away. Her mouth grew dry. She didn't want Emily to take over her mind either, but she didn't see any other option.

"I don't think I have any other options. She will know where they went. At least we will have some warning before she does it and you will be there to watch over me. It'll be okay."

His shoulders slumped as he exhaled. "Okay, but I don't like it. I don't even like you getting out of this car. We don't know where they are or if they have guns."

Flashing Tate a grim smile, Hazel reached out and quietly opened the door. A thin breeze blew across her face as she rose onto her legs. A nearby storm threatened to drench them, but she made her way across the lawn to the awaiting spirit.

Tate followed her, but left some distance, so Emily wasn't scared away. The spirit of Emily turned to face her as she got close, eyeing Tate warily but not vanishing at the sight of him. Approaching her gingerly, Hazel scanned the tree line, looking for anyone who may have been visible in the distance, but all she saw was wilderness.

"I hoped you would come," Emily said as she moved closer to Hazel. Hazel swallowed back the taste of fear that had grown in her throat.

"Show me."

Emily nodded before placing her hands on the side of Hazel's face. Tate held onto her as everything went black.

***

The swamp passed beneath her feet as she flew through the trees. Her feet not touching the ground. All was quiet except for the trill of the frogs and chirp of the crickets. She scanned left and then right, looking for signs of life, signs of people. Three officers trudged through the mud up ahead, guns in their hands as they walked. Her stomach rolled as she coasted, knowing her husband was in danger.

As she arrived at the location of Joshua and Hunter in the marsh, she dropped down to follow them on foot. She didn't know where they were going, but she knew they shouldn't be there, not with weapons anyway. Approaching a line of camps along the water, the men slowed as they crouched down behind the foliage. She moved past them to get a better look. A few buildings lined the water's edge, but the properties were quiet. She could not imagine what Joshua was expecting to see out there. Maybe a man in a swamp monster costume? That was the only thing that made any sense. Unless he believed he knew who the killer was, but she didn't think that was the case. Just as she turned to go back to her husband's side, movement from the trees behind him startled him upright.

***

"Hazel... are you okay?" Tate pet her hair gently as she woke from Emily's spirit-induced memory. She laid on the ground with her head on his lap.

"Yeah... I think so."

Leaning over, Tate kissed her on the nose. "Did you see anything?"

She looked in Emily's direction, but the spirit was gone. Hazel nodded her head sleepily. "The police caught up to him. He was staking out some camps on the river. Emily suspected he was looking for the man in the swamp monster costume."

Sounds near the swamp's edge drew their attention as the group of men crossed the small bridge and arrived back at the Landry's yard. The police had Joshua and Hunter in handcuffs. The detective waved a hand at Hazel and Tate before making the way to his car. Joshua locked eyes with her for the first time, sending shivers down her body. The look in his eyes was pure rage, making her insides turn. She had never seen his face contort in such a way.

She and Tate watched as the detective and fellow police officers walked Joshua and his friend to the cruisers in handcuffs, wrote them a ticket, spoke to them for a few minutes, and then took off their handcuffs and let them go on their way. Hazel's mouth dropped in disbelief.

"I wonder why they're letting them go," she said, turning to look at Tate, who was now sitting next to her on the grass.

He cleared his throat as he threw a clover he was playing with back into the grass. "He's probably trying to prevent any more backlash. With the stink Joshua has been creating publicly, another arrest would only strengthen his cause."

Hazel nodded, although the entire situation made her uncomfortable. "Are you ready to go home? I guess I have to stop and get my car from the station, though."

Tate kissed her on the forehead before helping her to her feet. "Yeah. Let's go home. It's going to rain soon, anyway."

Having spent most of the time since they'd arrived in the yard unconscious, Hazel had forgotten about the dark clouds moving over the area. Just as she began to walk to Tate's car, the first of many raindrops began to fall against her skin. They picked up the pace as the onslaught of rain became heavier.

"I'm going to call you later," Detective Bourgeois called out as he slid down into his own car. Tate nodded before opening the car door for Hazel and running to get into his spot before becoming drenched by the afternoon storm.

Joshua Landry watched them as they backed out of his driveway. His eyes were trained on Hazel the entire time, making her skin crawl.

"I want to stop by my old apartment." Hazel looked down as she spoke, fiddling with the buttons on her shirt. Something told her to look for Malerie, and it was the only place she thought she could find her. She had sent Candy to look for Malerie but wasn't sure if the spirit would even speak to Candy. She had to see her for herself .

Tate cleared his throat before clasping his hand around hers. "Don't you think you should maybe wait? You've been through a lot today. I know visions like that take a lot out of you."

"No... I don't feel like I have the luxury of time.

We need a break in this case. I'll look for her in the parking lot. If she's not there, then I'll go home. I just feel like I have to try."

Tate insisted on going with her to look for Malerie's spirit, so they went to her old apartment before picking up her car. They arrived at the apartment complex just before dark. Tate parked in her old parking spot and agreed to wait in the car while she walked around. It was unlikely Malerie would appear if he were with her.

"Don't go too far. It's getting dark, and this city isn't exactly safe." Tate squeezed her hand gently before pulling her in for a kiss.

"I won't. I promise."

The rain had become a light drizzle by the time she opened the car door to climb out. A siren in the distance caught her attention. She wrapped her arms around her chest, stroking her arms as she made her way to the building's entrance. The last time she had seen Malerie, both times she had seen her, the spirit stood in the parking lot of the building. She hoped this night would be the same. Not seeing the spirit initially, she sat down on the front stoop of the building, scanning the surrounding area for anyone who may be nearby.

A chill in the air brought her senses on high alert. Every sound blared into her ear. Dripping water from the gutters, a dog a few blocks away, the cars on a nearby highway, and that damn siren pulled her attention in different directions, nearly making her miss the form that had manifested on the step next to her.

Suddenly scared to look beside her, Hazel kept her eyes pointing downward. Malerie's tennis shoes lay beside her own shoes, as though she were a person with a corporeal body. Mud caked the formerly white pair just as mud caked Hazel's flats.

"He took her," the spirit said. Her voice sounded far away, although she was sitting so close. "There's still time. She's still alive."

A sudden feeling of cold filled Hazel's core, freezing her heart until it hurt. She had a feeling Michelle was still alive, and now she knew for sure.

"Where is she? How can I find her? Who has her?"

"He has her near the river. I don't know who

he is. He wore a mask when he came into the shack. He blindfolds us until we get inside."

"Can you show me?"

Malerie's head tilted to one side as she looked at Hazel thoughtfully. "I'm not sure how."

Hazel hesitated, biting her lip. "I'm not sure either. Some spirits are able to touch me and concentrate on the memory to send it to me. I'm not sure how it works."

Malerie shrugged before reaching for Hazel's arm. Hazel flinched but held still. "I can try."

As soon as Malerie's spectral hand hit Hazel's skin, an icy shiver traveled up her arm and throughout her body. She waited for the blackness to consume her, for the visions to flood in, but nothing happened. She closed her eyes and tried to force sleep, but it was impossible to do while she sat on a cold concrete step and listened to traffic in the distance. Malerie noticed her grimace and pulled away.

"I guess it's not working?"

Hazel rubbed warmth back into her arm while she shook her head. "Apparently not."

"There isn't much more time for her. I'm not sure why he hasn't killed her yet, but he will."

Confirmation of what Hazel already knew tightened an already present knot in her stomach. "I know."

A vibration in Hazel's pocket startled her. She clumsily fumbled, trying to grab her phone. A message from Tate waited on the screen. Using her face recognition, she unlocked the screen to read the message.

"Are you okay?" it read. "I just received a call from Detective Bourgeois. They started to stakeout Aberdeen's home and business. No sign of Michelle yet, but they are keeping a close eye. Please come back soon."

Glancing at the spirit beside her, Hazel responded to Tate, assuring him she was okay, before placing her phone back into her pocket.

"Malerie... I was curious why you have been staying near this apartment. Was it because I lived here?"

Malerie's face held a blank expression when she looked up from fumbling with the hem of her dress.

"You lived here?" she asked incredulously. "I've been here because I lived here."

The knot in Hazel's stomach tightened,

making it hard to swallow, hard to breathe. Even if Malerie was taken from her parents' fishing cabin in Honey Island Swamp, what were the chances he took someone living in her building. The coincidence created a physical reaction in her body. The dread took over as she imagined one worst case scenario after another. She curled into herself, wrapping her arms tightly around her chest as she rose onto shaky legs.

"I'm sorry, Malerie. I have to go. I'll come back to see you soon."

Running back to Tate's car, and climbing in, slumped into the seat as she sucked in gasping breaths that didn't seem to want to come. He reached out to hold her and she let him. She desperately wanted comfort and safety, both of which he could give.

"It's okay, Hazel. It's okay, baby. Tell me what happened. I've got you." He petted her hair gently as she fought to take in air and cycle it through her lungs. Her breathing became more stable as she focused on the sensation of him rubbing her hair.

"Malerie lived here! Tate... what if he followed her from here? What if he was looking for me?"

She felt his body stiffen with her words, but he continued to caress her hair, cooing calming words into her ear.

"Lived where, sweetie? Where did Malerie live?"

Hazel sucked in a sobbing breath, blowing it out slowly. "She lived here, in my apartment complex. Didn't you know?"

His head shook against hers. "I didn't know. I'm sorry. Please don't think he was looking for you. Don't think like that. You're safe. You don't live here anymore. It's okay. We'll catch him."

She nodded her head, but she wasn't convinced. If the killer had any connection to Raymond Waters, like Peter Aberdeen did, there's a chance he knew about her killing Waters, and that made her a target.

"How about we leave your car at the precinct tonight and you ride home with me? Do you want to do that?"

Sitting up in her seat, Hazel grabbed a napkin out of the glove box and wiped her cheeks. "It's okay. I'll bring my car home. I don't want anything to happen to it."

He searched her face, making sure she had

collected herself enough to drive before kissing her on the cheek and putting his seatbelt back on. "Only if you're sure. Well, let's get you home. Are you ready?"

"Yeah. I'm okay. Let's go home."

After picking up her car from the police department, she followed Tate to their home in the suburbs of downtown. Instinctually, Hazel glanced in the rearview mirror many times while she drove out of the city, but she tried to pay attention to the road. Traffic had thinned out while they were at her old apartment, so there weren't as many cars on the road. Her emotions calmed down, leaving a sense of resignation behind. She had been in the sights of many killers over her life, so one more didn't tip the scales. As long as he didn't succeed in killing her where the others had failed. She grimaced at her own assessment of the situation. Over the lonely drive home, she reflected on everything that happened over the past few months and decided she needed to call in reinforcements. She needed to call her mother.

17

Spiritual
Cavalry

Hazel gnawed on her lip as she held the phone in her hand. She'd been sitting that way for nearly fifteen minutes, not dialing the phone, just staring at it. Tate walked into his office, setting a glass of sweet tea in front of her.

"Have you called her yet?"

She flicked her eyes up at him, startled by his presence. "Sorry. I was in my own little world. Thank you for the tea. No... I haven't called yet."

"Can I get anything for you? Do you want me

to call out for Candy? I assume she's in here somewhere." He flashed an assuring smile before placing a kiss on her forehead.

"No. I have to do this by myself. It's my fault for not talking to her in forever."

"Okay, love. Call me if you need me. You've got this." He gave her one more kiss before leaving the room, quietly shutting the door behind himself.

She returned her stare to the phone in her hand, finger scrolling through her contacts but pausing when she saw the entry for her mother. She didn't know why she was hesitating so much. She did not speak to her mother much, but they had never had a falling out. It was her father who she had a rift with, and he wasn't the one she was calling. Taking in a deep breath and blowing it out slowly, she tapped the contact and watched in horror as the call began to dial.

After only one and a half rings, the voice of a woman answered the phone. She knew that voice anywhere; it was her mother.

"Hazel?"

A few awkward seconds passed before Hazel found the ability to respond.

"Mom?"

"Hazel, are you okay?"

Tapping her finger nervously, tears began falling down her cheek as the floodgates opened.

"Mom... there's a lot I need to tell you."

The words came out unabated. Hazel told her mother everything, from her friendship with Candy, to her engagement, to the series of spirit-led cases she's been involved in that had put her in the midst of a murderer. Finishing her monologue about the current case, where an innocent woman was still alive but wouldn't be for long, she asked her mother for help. She didn't know what that help would entail, but she did not care. Before ending their call, her mother offered to fly to New Orleans and help her with the investigation. Relief flooded over her.

Part of her was terrified of introducing her mother to her life in the south, but the other part of her was relieved. She wouldn't have to shoulder the full weight of the victims' spirits anymore. Her mother had the same abilities as she did, so her mother's light would shine just as brightly, attracting spirits to her, too. She could get so much farther with the support of someone else like her, and she wouldn't be so scared to venture out into territories that usually traumatized her. Now she just needed to tell Tate and Candy about her mother's visit. That part made her nervous.

Walking out of Tate's office, she could hear the news playing on the television, so she figured Tate was probably waiting for her on the sofa. Deciding to make a stop at Candy's bedroom first, she knocked lightly on the door. Hearing noises from inside of the room, she hesitated to walk in uninvited.

"Come back later, Hazel." Candy called out through the door. Realizing exactly what was going on in there, she smirked.

"Ewe," she said as she walked away, still shaking her head.

Sneaking around the back of the sofa, she intended to scare Tate while he wasn't expecting her, but he was asleep, so she decided to wake him slowly instead. Moving around to the front of the sofa, she watched him sleep for a few moments. He looked so peaceful when he slept, and deliciously handsome. Gently crawling on top of him, she noticed the corner of his mouth twitch, like he may have been starting to smile, but his eyes remained closed. She thought he may have been pretending to still be sleeping, but she played along. It only took a few lingering kisses on his neck for him to wake up fully.

"Oh... hey," he said sleepily. "I could get used to this."

She giggled, resting her chin on his chest. "I'm not even so sure that you were really sleeping."

His eyebrows lifted in amusement as a wide grin spread across his lips. "Is that so?"

Covering her face, Hazel started to laugh harder. "Oh my gosh, Tate. I totally think Candy and Jake are in there doing it. I knocked, and she totally blew me off. I don't understand the physics of how that even works." She tried to stifle her giggles, but failed. Tate chuckled in return before trying to muster a stern face.

"In my house? That's it. She's grounded. Candy!"

Placing her finger against his lips, they both started to laugh harder. "Shh! Don't interrupt them. We don't want her to start disrupting us."

"Fair point. Do you think she heard me?"

"No," Hazel laughed. "I hope not."

"You're in a good mood. Phone call went well?"

Hazel's giggles stopped as she rolled onto her side and wedged herself between Tate and the back of the sofa. He turned to face her, playing in her hair.

"I told her everything. I couldn't help it. It was like word vomit."

"Well... you haven't spoken to her in a long time. I'd imagine you had a lot to tell her, anyway. I'm just glad she answered the phone. You seem lighter now, like you aren't carrying so much on your shoulders."

Hazel nodded as she began to trace circles on his chest with her fingers. "Yeah. I feel lighter. I do have something to tell you, though. I hope it's okay."

"Oh. I'm sure it is... whatever it is." Leaning towards her, Tate kissed her on her nose, causing her to blush.

"My mom is coming to visit. She's going to help me with this case. She's flying in tomorrow."

He nodded. It was like he expected it. "Good. I figured you were going to ask her to come. I'm glad she's willing and able."

"You're okay with it?"

"Of course I am. She's your mom. Hopefully she likes me, though. We will have to figure out where she will stay and stuff, but I'm glad you're reconnecting with her. Hey... maybe she can take you to look at wedding dresses."

Reaching around her, Tate pulled her in for a tight hug. She closed her eyes and sank into his warmth.

"You guys rang?" asked Candy as she landed on Hazel's back like a spider monkey, making the warm embrace feel like it had been covered in an ice bath.

"Candy... can you get off of me?" Hazel struggled to get her words out under Candy's spectral body. Candy disappeared, reappearing in the chair next to the sofa. "Thank you."

"Uh... I'll go shower," Tate said as he climbed off the sofa. "Will you be in soon?" Hazel nodded as he left the room.

"So, what's up?" asked Candy as she watched Tate leave the room.

"Were you and Jake..."

"Yes."

"Nuff said. Where is he?" Hazel gazed around the room but didn't see Jake anywhere.

Candy's lips rose into a mischievous smile. "He's resting. You know how his energy is. He can power through... but then he has to rest."

"Okay, that was more than I needed to know. I was just going to tell you I called my mom, and she's coming to visit."

"Really?"

"Really."

Candy clapped her hands, bouncing on her seat. "Yay! I'm so excited to meet her! She'll be able to see me, right?"

"Yes."

"Yes! This is going to be so exciting! How long is she staying?"

Hazel's excitement was not on par with Candy's, but she was happy to see Candy looking forward to something. "I'm not sure. She's coming to help with the missing person's investigation."

"Ooh! Maybe we can go buy a wedding dress for you too!"

Hazel's eyes rolled as Candy continued to cheer in her chair. "You sound just like Tate. I'd swear the two of you are more excited about the wedding dress shopping than I am."

"That just means we have to get you excited!"

"You can try. Well... I'm going to go take a shower and head to bed. See you in the morning. Love you."

Candy blew her a kiss as she got up from the couch and made her way to the bedroom door. "Love you too, doll."

Hazel entered the bedroom just as Tate was getting out of the shower. He winked at her as he was drying his hair with a towel, wearing only boxer shorts. She licked her lips, closing the distance between them, and wrapped her arms around him. The kiss he planted on her lips made her knees buckle and stole the breath from her lungs. It was hard to pull away and take a bath, instead of jumping in bed with him, but she felt disgusting after her day and didn't want to torture him by being against her body for longer than was necessary.

Instead of leaving her to shower alone, he ran a bubble bath for her and sat on a chair near the tub, pouring the warm water over her and keeping her company.

By the time she attempted to fall asleep that night, she was exhausted, but her mind buzzed around her mother's visit and the investigation that had taken over her life. She hadn't been around her enough in the past eight years to even know the status of her mother's abilities. She could have weakened over the years, or she could be more powerful than she was before. Hazel didn't have a clue. All she knew was that her mother wanted to help, and believed she could, so Hazel hoped they could solve the case together. Hopefully, before it was too late for Michelle's life.

When Hazel fell asleep, it was fitful. Her mind stayed awake while the rest of her body rested.

***

A jolt startled me awake as I came back from the darkness inside of my mind and found a similar darkness in waking. My eyes were hidden behind a bandana roughly wrapped around my head. I couldn't see much but, beneath my bare arms, I could feel what was unmistakably a vehicle's thin, cushion-less carpeting. I could not remember how I had gotten there, but I was in a trunk. Even though I couldn't see them, the walls began to close in on me and the air seemed to thin. My lungs burned from the lack of oxygen, and I panicked, beating my bound hands and feet on any surface I could reach. It didn't budge, but it felt better to fight than to lie there helpless.

The car hit a pothole, causing my head to bang against the roof of the trunk. A scattering of white spots replaced my former view of blackness. It sparkled like the night sky, but without the same magic. I cried out in pain as my head throbbed, but there was no one there to help me, no one to care. Closing my eyes, I tried to calm down my breathing, but the air continued to become thinner. I didn't know whose car I was trapped in, or how long I had been there, but I tried to remember anything I could about how I had gotten there.

Trying to get some rest and fresh air, I had traveled to my parents' fishing camp on Honey Island to stay for a few days. It was my favorite place to go as a child, so I knew it was exactly what I needed after the busy month I'd had. I remembered fishing on the deck but being startled by something in the swampland's trees. Something large stalked through the marsh, setting its eyes on me. I shuddered at the thought of it and began trying to untie my hands and feet again, but it was no *use. They were bound too tight. The vehicle slowed as it drove over uneven terrain, but the more it slowed, the more my heart raced. The blood pulsed in my ears, overwhelming my senses and making it hard to think.*

As the vehicle pulled to a stop, I held my breath as I listened to the driver exit the car and the ground slosh and crunch under their feet. Twilight came into the crack as the door opened, revealing the shadow of a monster. My chest tightened, and I struggled to scream, but a burning sensation in the side of my neck stifled my scream and brought unconsciousness upon me once again.

***

The alarm clock wailed as Hazel slept, the sound playing into her dreams until the snooze kicked in automatically. Upon the sounding of the follow-up alarm, it achieved its job, startling her away. She frantically tried to turn the alarm off, but only snapped a picture of the screen by accident. It took multiple attempts before the alarm was silenced. By that time, she was fully awake.

Wiping the sleep from her eyes, she squinted into the screen of her phone for a few clueless moments before realizing she would be late for her drive to the airport to pick up her mother if she didn't climb out of bed immediately. Tate had already left for work, so at least she wouldn't have any distractions keeping her under the covers instead of moving on with her day. Dragging herself out of bed, she trudged into the bathroom and splashed water on her face.

The bags under her eyes revealed just how poorly she had slept. The nightmare that consumed her night was traumatizing. The emptiness inside of her stomach was still there as she dabbed concealer over the darkness above her cheeks. She guessed the memory had been from Malerie, especially after their discussion the night before, but the memory didn't show her anything new. She still jotted the details of the memory down once she left the bathroom, just as Celeste had instructed her, but she didn't know that it had given her any new insights into what happened to the murdered woman.

"Morning, roomie," Candy said from just inside the doorway. "Are you almost ready to go?"

Hazel shot her a sideways glance as she closed

her notebook and placed it back into the drawer in her bedside table. "Only if you don't embarrass me. My mom can actually see you, you know... and hear your dirty mouth."

Candy smirked, twirling her impossibly long red locks playfully. "I know, doll. That's the best part. I won't embarrass you. Your mom and I will be great friends. I just know it."

"If you say so. Yeah... we need to head out."

Throwing her bag over her shoulder, they exited the house and jumped into Hazel's car. Nausea rose in her stomach as she made the short drive to the airport. After not seeing her mother for years, she didn't know what to expect from the visit. She hoped they would continue from the day she left New Mexico, but she knew that was unlikely. As she parked her car in the short-term parking lot at the airport, her anxiety intensified.

Candy moved in close to Hazel as they walked into the building, wrapping an icy spectral hand around Hazel's waist. "Don't be nervous, doll. This is a good thing. She's your mom. You don't have to worry so much."

Hazel nodded, not that the pep talk improved

her anxiety by much. "I know... I just haven't seen her in so long, or spoken to her before last night, so I'm still a bit nervous."

"That makes sense... well, I'm excited for the two of you. It'll be good to be reunited."

Hazel's mother, Sandi, agreed to meet her near the baggage claim area of the airport, so she headed that way at once. Grabbing a spot in one of the seating areas, she watched as the crowd of people poured in from the terminals. A familiar mane of dark hair separated from the crowd as her mother approached, rolling a small suitcase beside her. Tears streamed down Hazel's cheek as her mother's face lit up when she saw her. Her mother's pace increased until they wrapped their arms around each other.

"Hazel, you look so good." Sandi's voice was choked as she squeezed Hazel tightly. "Oh, I've missed you."

Nausea in Hazel's belly was replaced by buzzing bees as her mother held her. "I missed you too. Thank you for coming."

Pulling away so she could look at Hazel's face, Sandi smiled genuinely. "Thank you for calling!"

Without looking away from Hazel, Sandi smiled at Candy. "So, is this the best friend?"

Before Hazel could respond, Candy moved in and hugged them both. "I am the BFF and I'm so glad to meet you, Mrs. Sandi!"

Grabbing her mother's suitcase handle, Hazel points towards the baggage claim. "We should get the rest of your luggage and head to the car so you two can get to know each other without so many people around."

"I agree," Sandi said. "I'm afraid if I don't grab it now, the staff may put it in the lost and found. I'll be right back."

Hazel's mother approached the shrinking crowd around the carrousel while she and Candy stood back and waited.

"Your mom's really pretty," said Candy. "I see where you get it from."

"Awe... thanks. Why are you buttering me up, Casper?"

"Not buttering, doll. Just speaking the truth... if only you'd wash your hair more."

Hazel rolled her eyes. "Hey! I wash my hair way more since Tate and I got together."

"Thankfully... he may not have proposed, if not."

Just as Hazel let out a loud gasp, her mother approached with a larger suitcase and a beaming smile.

"You girls ready to go? I don't know about you, Hazel, but I'm starving."

"We can grab something to eat. What do you have in mind, Mom?"

"I'm open to any location that has good Cajun cuisine!"

"Say no more," said Candy. "My treat."

Sandi looked at Candy in confusion, but the three of them began walking in the parking garage's direction. Hazel snickered. "Well, Candy. If you're paying, I'm up for any location, too."

Arriving at her car, Hazel opened the door for her mother before putting the luggage in the trunk. Elation, that she only usually felt with Tate seemed to flurry to life as she climbed into the car. She did not realize how much she had missed her mother until she laid eyes on her again. She knew, without any doubt, that her mother had reentered her life to stay, and that was a happy thought.

"Oh!" Sandi turned to face her as soon as Hazel dropped into the driver's seat. "You didn't show it to me!"

Hazel's head titled in confusion. "Show you what?"

"Your engagement ring!" Her mother pulled her left hand across the center console of the car to take a closer look at the ring Tate had given to her. Excited to be involved, Candy leaned over the center console, from her space in the backseat, and eyed the ring as well, with a dreamy look on her face.

"Oh, this is beautiful, Hazel," said Sandi. "He must be some guy. I can't wait to meet him."

"Thanks, Mom. He looks forward to meeting you, too. He will be home from work around dinnertime, so you won't have to wait long."

Sandi smiled warmly as she released Hazel's hand and buckled her seatbelt. "Well, ladies... are we ready for lunch?"

They both responded "yes," although Candy had no use for food. Placing the car in drive, they

exited the parking garage and drove towards the
city.

18

Combining Worlds

Offering to pay for their lunch out of the large amount of money she had hidden in boxes that now lived in Tate's office safe, Candy chose one of her favorite Cajun restaurants near the city. Although she couldn't eat the food herself, she wanted to properly introduce Sandi to the food that had become well-known around the world. Hazel could never imagine paying so much for lunch, but she wasn't paying.

Ordering several dishes for her and her

mother to share, as well as a spicy Bloody Mary for Sandi, the three of them listened to the Zydeco music while waiting for the server to bring their food. The rich scent of Cajun cuisine filled the air, only making them hungrier.

"So," Sandi said, leaning closer to Hazel. "Tell me a little more about this case you're needing help with. What do I need to know?"

Pulling her chair closer to her mother so they could hear each other over the background music, Hazel proceeded to tell her mother everything about the case, from her first introduction to Malerie Ledet outside of her apartment months earlier, to the arrest and release of Joshua Landry. Sandi listened with eyes wide, nodding every few minutes in acknowledgement, but she didn't interrupt.

Just as Hazel finished her story, their server arrived with their lunch. Large, overfilled plates of steaming Cajun food were placed in the center of the table, with two empty plates put in front of Hazel and Sandi, so they could portion out the food they were sharing. Candy floated near the food dreamily, waving her spectral hands through the steam, trying to force the scent into her ghostly nose.

"Oh, this smells amazing, but I have no idea what any of this delicious food is. Care to tell me what I'm eating?" Sandi began shoveling food from the several plates into her empty one, whether or not she knew what the mysterious items were.

Doing the same, Hazel pointed out what the items were as she spooned her own servings. "These are clearly oysters, but they are charbroiled. So, they broil the shucked oysters after they're topped with seasonings, cheese, and butter. I usually eat them on crackers, and they are amazing." Setting aside the plate of oysters, Hazel grabbed a heaping plate of creamy pasta and plopped a large helping of it on her plate. "This pasta dish is topped with crab cakes and eggplant. It's one of my favorites. The crabmeat is mixed with lots of herbs and seasoning and breadcrumbs and then deep fried with the eggplant. The sauce is a dairy-based cream sauce." Pushing the plate of pasta aside and pulling the last plate towards her, Sandi looked at it expectantly. The last plate contained a rice dish with large chunks of vegetables and grilled shrimp. "This last dish is called jambalaya. The rice is seasoned with a lot of different seasonings, and I admittedly don't know all of them, but I can say that it's delicious."

Candy nodded as she leaned over the table, clearly longing for a bite she couldn't take.

As they began eating, Sandi's audible moans of delight revealed just how much she liked the food. She didn't respond to Hazel's explanation of the case until she pushed away her plate and discreetly unbuttoned her pants to give her stomach more room. Hazel and Candy both snickered.

"Well," Sandi muttered. "That was delicious, and I think I need stretch pants now." Hazel nodded as she forced the last few bites of her food into her mouth. "As far as your case is concerned, when do you want to go back to the swamp?"

Hazel nearly choked. She had never intended to return to the swamp, although she knew why her mother wanted to go. "Um... I guess we can go tomorrow. Do you have any ideas about what we will do when we get there?"

"I think we need to see where that husband is going when he goes into the woods with his gun, and I hope to be able to speak to his wife."

The familiar knot in the pit of Hazel's stomach returned. Not only did her mother want to return to the swamp, but she wanted to hike deep into it. "Okay... but I'd rather not go into the swamp without some sort of protection. I'm going to ask Tate to come with us, just in case we happen upon anyone while we are in there. The swamp can be a dangerous place, but that goes without saying about the reasons we are going there in the first place. I don't want us to go in there alone."

Sandi nodded, taking the last sip of her cocktail. "That's a good plan. My only fear would be that the spirits won't talk to us with him there, but I guess it's worth the risk."

Hazel thought about her mother's concern before responding. "It's a valid concern, but I have to say that Emily has become less shy over time. The last time she spoke to me, Tate was next to me the entire time. I think she realizes he comes with the package. I don't think his presence will make a difference to her."

"Then it's settled. Well... should we get the rest of this food to go?"

Nodding, Hazel motioned to the server and asked him for some boxes to take their food home. He came back quickly, picking up their payment and dropping off Styrofoam boxes. After securing their remaining food into containers, the three women left for the journey back home.

The decision was made that Sandi would bunk up in Candy's room during her stay. It was the only open bedroom since the third room was Tate's office and didn't have a bed. Candy was excited about the company. Even though she had a spirit boyfriend, Jake, his lack of energy control meant he didn't stay around as often as she would have liked, so she still spent a good bit of time alone. Since Hazel took a break from working, she and Candy had been able to spend more time together. However, Hazel had been working with the police department, and she had a live-in boyfriend, so she didn't have as much time to spend with Candy as Candy would have liked.

Hazel's nerves wound up steadily the closer it

got to Tate getting off work. Her mother meeting Tate was something she knew would happen eventually, but she didn't think it would happen so soon. Tate would impress her mother, of course, but it would still be combining her present with her past, and it wasn't something she had expected to do. Sandi appeared equally nervous about meeting Tate. She was so antsy about it she insisted on preparing dinner for him. Hazel thought she just had too much energy to sit still, but she didn't argue. At least one of them could cook.

Leaning over the sink and washing vegetables, in an effort to at least be a small part of the cooking process, Hazel stared out of the window at the encroaching storm clouds. Candy floated alongside her, watching the sky as well.

"Looks like the sky is about to fall," Candy said, as she settled onto the countertop. She tended to sit as though she had a corporeal form.

"Yeah... I'm just hoping Tate gets home before it starts. I don't like anyone driving in these storms. It's dangerous."

Just as she spoke, the door from the garage swung open and Tate walked in.

"Tate!" Sandi dropped what she was doing and rushed to Tate, pulling him into a hug. His eyes grew wide as he sent a questioning glance to Hazel. She smiled and nodded her head.

"Nice to meet you, Mrs. Sandi," Tate said as he hugged Hazel's mother, patting her on the back. She had to stand on the tips of her toes to get her arms around Tate's tall, muscular frame.

"You're tall," Sandi said as she returned to her flat feet, which put her nearly a foot shorter than Tate.

Seeing an in, as her mother returned to the stove, Hazel ran up to Tate and wrapped her arms around him.

"Hey there," he said as he kissed her. "Have a good day?"

Hazel smiled broadly as she nodded her head.

He squeezed her one last time before beginning his walk to the bedroom. "I'm going to get changed. I'll be right back."

As Tate left the room, Sandi's face grew into an animated grin. She turned to look at Hazel. "You've done well, Hazel. He's quite a man!"

Hazel blushed, partially hiding her face with her hand. "Mom... geez... I know."

"I've seen him naked too, so I fully agree," Candy chimed in. Hazel tried to throw a rag at her, along with the meanest face she could muster, but Candy vanished and reappeared across the room. She shrugged. "What? Don't be mad at me. It wasn't my fault that time."

"You just so happened to follow him into the men's locker room and didn't expect him to change... sure." Hazel rolled her eyes and returned to the vegetables in the sink.

The rain had begun pelting the window in front of her as the sky darkened below the tumultuous clouds. She thought about the night Candy followed Tate around before they had started seeing each other, so she could determine if he was good enough for Hazel. It was the same night Candy discovered how to send messages through Tate's police scanner, which had become a really helpful skill when Hazel got abducted by Raymond Waters. She shivered at the thought and pushed it from her mind, turning with the tray of vegetables and bringing them to Sandi by the stove.

They were making a vegetable pasta, one of her mother's specialties. She hadn't had her mother's cooking in nearly a decade, so it brought back a sense of nostalgia to be in the kitchen with her mother again.

"I never did ask about Dad, or Jason and Terry. How are they?" Hazel took over stirring the pot as her mother dug through the spices.

"Oh... they don't change much. Terry's wife just had a baby boy. They named him Jayden. I'll have to show you a picture later. He's a chunky little thing. Your dad had to get on blood pressure medication last year. Serves him right with all his stressing about things that don't concern him. Jason is married to his career, so he got divorced a few years back and hasn't settled down again. You should come back west soon. I know they would all love to see you."

An emptiness developed in Hazel's chest as she thought about her estranged family. She hadn't missed them until her mother told her about their lives. It brought memories flooding back of her time growing up with her brothers. How they would search for buried treasure on the family's property in New Mexico, or how their dad would take them on camping trips. Her relationship with them had become strained as her abilities became more pronounced and she moved further into herself as a result, but it didn't make her love them less. "Yeah. I'm sure the three of us can make our way over there eventually, especially since I'm not working anymore."

Noticing the expression on her face, Sandi turned and took Hazel by the hand. "I know it will be hard to come back after being gone for so long, Hazel, but I promise it'll be okay. Everyone loves and misses you, and they understand how much life gets in the way. Don't let that stop you from coming to visit. Okay?"

Hazel wiped an escaped tear from her cheek. "Okay."

"Whatever y'all are cooking smells great!" Tate walked back into the kitchen in a casual pair of sweatpants and a tee shirt. He approached the cabinet, pulling down three wine glasses. "Would you ladies like a glass of wine?"

Hazel wiped her cheek one more time before turning to face him. "Definitely a yes for me," she said before turning back to the pot she was stirring.

"Yes, for me too," said Sandi. She proceeded

to pour the boiled pasta into a colander that she placed inside the sink. "The food will be ready in about five minutes."

Sitting at the table for dinner, Tate and Sandi chatted a lot about his job and her life back in New Mexico. Hazel didn't speak much. She wanted them to get to know each other. After she felt like they had caught up properly, she brought up their plans for the next day.

"So, my mom wants to go back to the swamp tomorrow. Do you think you could come with us?"

Tate eyed her warily, arching an eyebrow as he always did. She smiled.

"Is that a yes?"

He nodded. "I did take tomorrow off so we could all spend the day together, so of course I can go with y'all, although I didn't think that was how y'all would want to spend your first full day together."

Hazel grimaced, chancing a look at her mother.

"It was my idea," said Sandi, setting her fork onto her plate. "It sounds like this murder case and missing person's investigation is pretty hot, so I figured we shouldn't waste any time."

"You're right," Tate nodded. "It's an unfortunate situation altogether and the police department can only do so much. Hazel's help has been invaluable to the department, though." He reached out and took Hazel's hand. She looked down at their interlocked fingers as he continued to speak. "Although I know it's been hard for her."

"I'm proud of her for helping with these difficult cases," Sandi added. Her voice was warm, and she looked down, trying to meet Hazel's eye. Hazel looked up from the table.

"Hopefully we can solve this case then," Hazel muttered, feeling less optimistic than the rest of them. She shrugged. "It doesn't feel like we are getting any closer to finding this guy, and time is running out for Michelle... if he hasn't killed her already."

Tate squeezed her hand gently. "Well, let's get to bed so we can solve this case tomorrow, then. Are you all set for your stay, Sandi?"

Hazel's mother nodded as she looked towards Candy. "Yes. I think between Candy and I, we have everything I need." Candy beamed at being included.

"I'll take care of my new mother. Don't y'all worry," Candy said, as she wrapped her arm around Sandi's shoulders.

Sandi made her way to take a shower before bed while Tate and Hazel rinsed and loaded the dishes into the dishwasher. A knot had settled permanently in Hazel's stomach after deciding to return to the swamp the next day and it adjusted in size throughout the night, growing larger the closer to bed they had gotten.

"Your mom seems happy to be here." Tate dried his hands as he turned to face Hazel, who had just finished rinsing the sink. He pulled her close to him, wrapping his arms around her waist. "You worried about tomorrow?"

Laying her face against his chest, she nodded. "You know me so well. I can't hide anything from you."

He snickered, kissing the top of her head. "I don't want you to hide anything from me, so I'm glad I can tell when you're feeling overwhelmed. That way, I can try to help you."

Leaning back so she could look into his face, she smiled bashfully. "You're quite good at it."

As he leaned into her and placed his lips against hers, she closed her eyes and vowed to let him try to get her mind off the day ahead. "Let's go to bed," he said as he wrapped his arm around her waist and escorted her to the bedroom door, closing the door gently behind them. The closing door separated Hazel from her worries for tomorrow. Instead, she allowed her senses to take in Tate's closeness. His scent and the taste of his kiss intoxicated her. His touch electrified her. When she fell asleep, her mind was far away from tomorrow. All it had room for was the man in her arms.

19

Shots in the Distance

Pacing the dirty wood planked floor of the shack, I debated my options. He had been gone for days. What if he didn't come back, and I starved to death in here? My stomach growled just as I thought about it, but the plate on the floor had been empty for two days. After a few days of no sounds outside, and no unwanted visits to my prison, I began to wonder if he was gone for good.

I tried to escape from the wooden structure repeatedly but had been unsuccessful. The bars on

292 C. A. Varian

the widows were solid, and the spaces between the bars weren't big enough for me to squeeze through. The door locked from the outside, and no amount of banging made it budge. I didn't know what else to do. I had lost track of how long I had been there, how long since he abducted me. No one knew I was here. If he returned, he'd probably kill me. If he didn't return, I'd probably starve. My breaths fell into a panicked quick rhythm as I began banging on the door, screaming for help, until I was battered and breathless on the floor.

***

Gasping, Hazel woke herself up in a struggle for breath. Tate hovered over her, a worried look on his face. "Calm down, baby. You're okay. I've got you."

Sitting down against the headboard, Tate pulled her against his chest and caressed her hair gently as she focused on pulling breath into her nose and blowing it out of her mouth. She ran her hand down her face, resting it across her mouth as she stifled back a sob, refusing to give it that much power over her.

"Who was it?" Tate asked.

"I'm not sure. I saw the shack again, but only the inside."

Rolling out of Tate's reach, she pulled her notebook and pen out of the side table drawer before returning to lean against his chest.

He resumed running his fingers through her hair. "Did you learn anything new from the vision?"

She thought about his question for a moment, closing her eyes to enjoy his caress. "He left her."

The movement of Tate's hand stopped. "What do you mean?"

"She was left undisturbed for several days and she didn't know why. She was afraid she would starve. She tried to get out of the building, but she couldn't."

Tate scratched at his chin before returning to his task of rubbing her hair. "That's strange. I mean... leaving her like that could have gotten him caught. I'm assuming he eventually returned, though."

"I'm assuming so, but I didn't see it. I woke up."

"Do you still want to go today?"

"Yes, honestly, the nightmares only make it

more urgent. I want to solve this case so I can stop dreaming about it. I'd give anything to just have dreams about you."

He pulled her back until he could kiss her on the lips. "Until you're able to have pleasant dreams, I will have to keep trying to give you wonderful waking memories."

Grabbing the back of his neck and pulling him into one more kiss, she smiled before sitting back up on the bed. "It's a deal... I guess we need to get ready to go though... although I could stay in bed with you all day."

Tate climbed out of the bed behind her, walking to the bathroom. "After this case is resolved, we will do just that."

They stopped for coffee and beignets on their return to the Honey Island swamp area. Thankfully, the storm clouds seemed to stay away from where they were heading because the last thing they wanted was to be stuck in the swamp in the rain. Even with decent enough weather, and a car full of people who supported her, Hazel still felt the pulsating knot in her stomach as she watched the city fade out of the car window and they crossed the bridge that took them towards their destination.

"I understand y'all want to go look around where Emily and her husband were, but we can't go into their yard, so we will have to park down the street and sneak onto the property. Hopefully Joshua doesn't see us."

Thinking about Joshua Landry catching them in the swamp only made Hazel's stomach knot bigger. There wasn't a lot about the situation that made her feel comfortable. But as they pulled the car alongside the shell covered road, she tucked that nervousness aside and unbuckled her seatbelt.

The morning air held the chill of fall, and the fog covered the ground like an eerie blanket hiding its secrets. After the storms from days before, the ground sloshed below their rubber boots. Thankfully, Tate had an extra pair of rain boots for Sandi to borrow, because any other shoes would not have been appropriate for the swamp even on a dry day.

"We will cut through the trees here," Tate whispered as he huddled close to Hazel and her mother. "And then sneak across the bridge that crosses into the swamp near Joshua's back yard. Hopefully, no one sees us, but these aren't private lands, so we are permitted to be here."

"As long as Joshua isn't running around with a shotgun again," Hazel scoffed. Tate grimaced.

"Yeah. Let's hope that doesn't happen."

"Mom, are you okay?" Hazel looked towards Sandi, who seemed to not be engaged in their conversation. She was scanning the forest. She turned to Hazel's question.

"I'm fine, dear. I was just feeling for spirit energies. This place is buzzing. Do you feel it?"

Although sure of her answer, Hazel closed her eyes and focused on the energy around her for a moment. For a land that was usually swarming with the sounds of life, not even a cricket chirped. The only sound pouring across the space was the hum of electricity. The pulses of energy made her slightly nauseated. It was her body warning her to go the other way, but she couldn't.

"Yes. I feel it and it makes me sick."

Sandi flashed her a sad smile as she reached out and rubbed Hazel's shoulder. "We are going to solve this thing, Hazel. And then you don't have to come out here again."

Hazel shrugged. "I hope so."

The trio, with Candy pulling up the rear, headed into the trees, trudging deeper into the marsh. A familiar sense of desperation and panic found its way into Hazel's consciousness as they crossed the small bridge over the waterway separating the land from the swamp. She didn't need to see her to know Emily was somewhere nearby.

"Hazel." Candy spoke softly. Hazel stopped walking to focus on what Candy was trying to say.

"Yeah?

Candy tried to look discreetly over her shoulder before facing back to Hazel. "Emily is following behind us. I thought you should know."

Peeking around Candy's form, Hazel could just barely see Emily's spectral body as she hovered behind a cluster of trees. Hazel nodded and moved closer to Tate.

"Emily's caught up with us. I'm going to go

talk to her. Maybe she can show us where Joshua has been going."

Tate nodded briskly. "Be careful."

Walking carefully to avoid tree roots and puddles, Hazel approached Emily's spirit, still partially hidden behind a tree. Hazel glanced behind and noticed that her mother remained behind with Tate. She wondered if she should have asked her to tag along. Emily's blue eyes followed her as she approached.

"You shouldn't be here," Emily said as Hazel got close enough to hear her. "It's not safe. Call the police."

Hazel's eyebrows furrowed as she glanced back at her group. "Call the police for what? What are you talking about?"

Heavy as a weight, Hazel's heart dropped as Emily seemed to reach for her. She stumbled, leaning forward to grasp the trunk of a tree as Tate darted towards her. Chaos spun in her head as Tate grabbed her and lifted her into his arms. She closed her eyes as he carried her back to where her mother and Candy waited.

"What happened?" Sandi's voice sounded frantic as she ran her hand along Hazel's cheek.

"I saw that spirit, but she's gone now. Did she do something to you?"

Hazel shook her head, although she was unsure of the correct answer. She didn't think Emily had done anything to her, but the sensation that hit her by the trees was overwhelming. It took over her body in a way she couldn't fight.

Just as Tate was setting Hazel back onto her feet, a boom echoed around them, causing a flock of birds to flutter out of the trees.

"A gunshot," Tate said. "We need to get back to the car. Now! Get low and move!"

Tate pulled out his cellphone and began whispering into the line and those alive in their group crouched and shuffled back along the path they had taken to get where they were.

"Candy," Hazel whispered. Candy floated in closer to her until they were nearly touching. Hazel kept walking towards the car while she spoke. "Make your way towards where the shot came from and try to see who fired. Let us know what's going on so we can update the police."

With barely a nod, Candy disappeared on the spot as Hazel continued to move through the trees. As they approached the crossing which would get them to the car, a gunshot rang out again. This time, it was closer. Sandi, leading the group, tripped on a vine and landed in the mud. Tate's hand flew up, telling them to stay still. Hazel's heart hammered in her chest as she panted. Tate approached Sandi gingerly as she pulled herself up from the ground. Her knees and hands were covered in mud.

"Are you okay to walk?" he whispered.

Sandi took a delicate step on her right leg and winced. "I think my ankle is sprained, but I'll be okay."

Tate's face tensed, but he nodded. "I can carry you if you can't walk, but let's try you walking first because we need to stay low. Let's go."

Looking both ways before leaving the cover of the trees, the trio crossed the bridge and returned to the forest on the other side of the waterway. No other gunshots sounded as they made their way to the car. Two police cars sped past Tate's car as they approached the street. They all climbed into the safety of the car as Tate put in a call to Detective Bourgeois. He put the call on speaker so they could all listen.

"Officer Cormier... Are y'all safe in the car?"

"Yes, sir. Any word on the gunshots?"

"Not yet. Two units were on their way to Joshua Landry's house. I'll be there soon. I was doing surveillance of Peter Aberdeen's property nearby, so I'll be there soon. Keep them in the car where they are safe. I don't need the situation becoming more complicated."

"Yes, sir."

Just as the phone clicked off, Tate jumped out of the car.

"Where are you going?" Hazel called after him. Her voice shook with fear.

"I have my uniform and everything in the trunk. They may need backup. I'm going down there. You need to stay here with your mom. I won't be long. I promise."

Unbuckling her seatbelt, Hazel opened her own car door. "Then I'm coming with you."

"Hazel," Tate walked around to her side of the car and lowered himself to her height. "Hazel, listen to me. Your mom is hurt. Stay with her. I'm trained for this sort of thing. I'm going to be okay. Detective Bourgeois and his partner will be here soon. I'm just going to offer my help until they get here."

Hazel slumped into her seat as her argument lost steam. She knew he was right, no matter how much she hated the danger his job sometimes entailed. "Please be careful and don't be long. Please."

"I won't. I promise." Kissing her on the cheek, Tate closed her door slowly and proceeded to change into his uniform on the side of the quiet street and jog in the direction of Joshua Landry's home. As soon as she could no longer see him in the distance, Hazel turned to face her mother, who was sitting in the back seat.

"Can you walk?"

Sandi's eyebrows drew together in a tight v. "Why? Hazel... he said to stay here. Wait, look out there... Candy's coming back."

Turning in her seat to peer out of the windshield, Candy's flowing mane of red hair was unmistakable as she approached the car from the tree line. She flowed in through the driver's side door, settling into the seat Tate had abandoned.

"Candy... hey what's going on over there?"

Hazel's heart continued to hammer, making her feel the need to escape from the car and run down the street to where Tate had gone.

"It's some kind of standoff, doll. Two men with guns are at each other. I think one lives in a house down there and the other one doesn't. I'm not sure why they are fighting."

Rubbing her forehead, Hazel tried to imagine who the other man could be. She knew Joshua Landry was involved, but why was he shooting at someone?

"What did the other guy look like?"

Candy shrugged. "He was tall. Looked pretty scruffy."

Hazel's heart seemed to double in speed. "The Honey Island Swamp Monster," she muttered.

Sandi leaned forward in her seat. "What did you say, Hazel?"

Ice flowed through Hazel's veins as she turned to face her mother. Her eyes refused to blink. "The Honey Island Swamp Monster."

The previous look of confusion on Sandi's face changed when realization hit her. Her hand rose to cover her mouth as her jaw fell open.

Opening her car door, Hazel jumped out of

the car and onto the street. "He won't even know we're there. We'll stay in the trees. I can't stay behind."

***

"Should I bother objecting?" Candy asked, as she exited the car. "Or will you just ignore me like you always do?"

"Do you even need to ask?" Hazel sighed, opening her mother's car door.

Taking only a moment to look at her as though she had lost her mind, Sandi joined her daughter on the street. "Don't make me regret this."

20

Saving Bella

With Candy in the lead, the three women began walking in the direction of Joshua Landry's house. They remained just inside the tree line, but close enough to the road so they could see Tate if he was passing to return to the car. The sound of another vehicle drew their attention, and they stopped walking so they could peer through the trees and spot the driver. Detective Bourgeois with another man were making their way to the house as well. They couldn't walk any faster, since Sandi had an injured foot, so they continued their trek onward.

Voices became more pronounced as they came around the curve that led them to the Landry's property. As the trees began to open, they huddled behind a group of them and tried to make out what was being said.

"We understand you're in a situation, Hunter. We just want to help." An officer spoke loudly through the closed door. Joshua Landry no longer held a gun as he stood next to Detective Bourgeois. His face was twisted with emotions Hazel couldn't make out. "We just want the release of Bella with no harm to her. She's an innocent child. You don't want to hurt her."

Hazel felt the bile grow in her throat as she slid to the ground under weakened legs. Sandi rushed to her side, pulling her hair out of her face as she retched in the grass. Why was Hunter holding a seven-year-old child hostage inside her home? Hazel's body trembled.

"Oh no," Candy said, as she began caressing Hazel's hair. The chill of her touch helped Hazel's nausea. "Tate heard you throw up, or he saw you, but he's walking over. He does not look happy."

Hazel was too sick to care if Tate was mad about her leaving the car. The air felt thin as her head hung inches from the ground.

"What are you doing..." Tate hesitated as he rounded the trees and saw Hazel crumpled on the ground. Dropping to his knees, he pulled her in to him. Her tears broke through as his body met hers.

"I'm sorry. I couldn't stay back there," she sobbed.

"Shh. I know. I've got you." Holding her against his chest, they rocked together gently.

"He's got Bella? Tate... what's going on?"

"Joshua claims Hunter killed Emily. Says he was closing in on his friend and Hunter confronted him... Hunter was afraid to get caught. A fight broke out and he held a gun to Bella's head and forced Joshua out of the house. It's been a stand-off ever since. The police are trying to get him to release the kid."

Sandi sank down next to them. "That's terrible. Have they seen the child? Do they know she's okay?"

Pulling out a tissue from his pocket, Tate wiped Hazel's cheeks. "They've seen no sign that she's been harmed. They believe she's tied up somewhere in the house."

Sniffling, Hazel forced herself back up into a sitting position. "I can find out."

Tate's face fell. "Hazel, no. I don't want you getting involved."

She bit her lip, setting her hand on his arm. "No. You don't understand. I'm not going to go in there in this form. If Emily has been in the house, she can show me."

He remained quiet for a moment, glancing back to where the police stood watching the house. "Do you see Emily?"

"On it," said Candy, as she disappeared.

"Candy's going to look for her."

"I don't like how she makes you feel, Hazel. She almost put you in the hospital before." Tate continued to run his fingers through her hair. His eyes were brimming with emotion.

"I can watch her," said Sandi. "I'll be able to watch the spirit. I don't have the same abilities as Hazel, but I can monitor what Emily is doing and interrupt the transfer if it appears to be too much for her."

Tate nodded sternly. Candy reappeared only minutes after leaving with the spirit of Emily Landry. Emily's face was drawn and tear-stained, making her blue eyes sparkle. Hazel reached out to her.

"Do you understand what we need to do?"

With one slow nod, Emily reached forward and wrapped Hazel into an icy black sleep.

***

He paced the room nervously, peering out of the window every few moments and mumbling to himself. An assault rifle hung over his shoulder as an ominous reminder of why he had come. He had come to silence Joshua.

Bella sat at her kid-sized table and chair set, coloring a picture of a princess. There were no ropes binding her. She hummed sweetly as she dug for a different color crayon, seemingly oblivious to what was transpiring outside the house.

Last time Hazel saw Bella in a memory, she could have sworn the little girl saw her. She didn't know how, but she believed Bella may have otherworldly powers. Testing her theory, Hazel moved closer to the tiny table, dropping herself into one of the chairs. The little girl continued to hum and color until Hazel reached towards her hand. Bella moved her hand in a wide arc to go around where Hazel's hand laid on the table. Hazel gasped.

"You can see me?"

Bella's eyes flicked up, but she continued to hum, returning her glance to the page and coloring happily. Setting her crayon down, she turned to look at Hunter, who was peeking out of the window from the side.

"Uncle Hunter... can I go to the bathroom?"

***

"Hazel?" Tate's voice broke through her dream. Hazel rubbed her eyes as she sat up. Four sets of wide eyes watched her, waiting for her to speak. She turned to look at Tate.

"Tell the detective that Bella isn't tied up. She's free to go to the bathroom and stuff. If they wait outside the bathroom window, they may find an opportunity to grab her, or get to him when she's out of the way. I'm going to send Emily to watch her. When she's out of the room, I'll let them know."

The size of Tate's eyes did not shrink, but he quickly rose from his spot on the ground and darted through the trees to speak to the detective. Sandi took his spot and wrapped her arms around Hazel. "You did a great job, Hazel. I'm proud of you."

She smiled, returning her eyes to Emily. "Go to her and watch her. Tell me when she's away from him and I'll send them after her."

Without even so much as a nod, Emily disappeared. Tate returned with another officer Hazel recognized.

"Lawsen... Sandi has an injured ankle. Can you help her to the car and I'll help Hazel," Tate said as he reached around Hazel's legs and picked her up like she was weightless.

"Where are we going?" Hazel asked.

"We are just bringing y'all to the detective's car, so you have easier access to him when Emily signals. Plus, I don't want you getting a tick out here."

"Good plan."

Sitting in the police car, Hazel anxiously awaited Emily's message. After about thirty minutes, Emily returned.

"She's returned to the bathroom," Emily said. "She knows what's going on. It's time."

Hazel nodded, climbing out of the car so she could relay the message. At Detective Bourgeois' command, a group of three officers headed around the side of the building to recover Bella while the unsuspecting Hunter Billiot remained in the main part of the house, readying himself for a fight.

As the three officers approached the bathroom window to rescue Bella, four other officers readied a battering ram at the front door, preparing to force themselves inside and arrest Hunter. After three thrusts against the wooden door, the team made their way into the house while the rescue team used the distraction to get Emily's daughter from the other side of the house.

As Hunter was escorted out of the house in handcuffs, he refused to answer questions from the detective.

Another team, stationed outside of Hunter Billiot's home, entered the shop on his property at the detective's command, finding a beaten and emaciated Michelle Barrilleaux. She was still alive, but just barely, and was rushed to the hospital. After searching Hunter's home and property, it was clear he was planning to end Michelle's life soon. A filled syringe sat on his kitchen table, and a realistic swamp monster suit hung in his hall closet.

21

Future
Plans

"You look gorgeous!" Candy's big blue eyes were dripping with tears as she floated around the wedding dress shop. Hazel shielded her face with her hand as she prepared an epic eye roll.

"I do not look gorgeous. This thing is too damn fluffy. Look at it!" Using her hands, she flared out the bottom of the dress. It sparkled in the shop's light.

"She's right, you know," said Sandi, who was

sitting on a posh white chaise lounge and sipping on a flute of champagne. "You look gorgeous."

Hazel smirked. "Is this my life now? You too teaming up on me?"

Floating towards the chaise and wrapping her arm around Sandi's shoulder, Candy shrugged. "What did you expect? Your mom likes me better."

Sandi shrugged and smiled mischievously. Hazel gasped and stormed off the pedestal. "I'm going to get another dress! A less fluffy one!"

***

The three women could not stop giggling for most of the drive home from the bridal shop. Sandi had downed three too many glasses of champagne, but that wasn't Hazel's excuse.

"I really love the dress you chose, Hazel. You are going to be a beautiful bride," said Sandi, smiling genuinely as Hazel drove.

"Thanks, Mom. I'm just glad you were able to come with me. What time is your flight tomorrow?"

Sandi sighed before relaxing her face into a frown as she scrolled on her phone. "Ten in the morning. I'm sad to leave. I'm going to miss you girls... and Tate. Please visit soon."

"We will, Mom. I promise."

***

Lying in bed after a day of wedding dress shopping, Hazel felt more optimistic than she could ever remember. Finding peace for Malerie, Emily, and Jessica allowed her to have more nights without nightmares than those with. She felt better rested, and more in love with Tate, if that was even possible. She gave him so many reasons for him to be angry with her, but he never showed it, not even once.

"You're too good to me," she said as she curled up into the crook of his shoulder. Leaning over, he planted a lingering kiss on her lips.

"That's not possible. So... now that you have a dress... any idea of when you want to get married?"

Scrunching up her face, she rubbed her hand across his bare chest while she pondered his question. Surely his muscles had magical powers and would give her the answer. "I'm thinking the sooner the better, before you change your mind about me."

He snickered, rubbing his hand along her back. "I will not change my mind about you, but I like how you think. The sooner the better works for me, too."

"But," she added. "I don't want a big wedding. I don't really know anyone in this city, anyway."

Turning onto his side, Tate pulled her against him, wrapping his arms around her waist. "So, what do you have in mind, then? After all the action we've had this year, I understand wanting to do something more intimate."

Grinning up at him, she ran her hand along his strong jawline.

"How about Vegas?"

He smirked, pulling her in tighter. "Vegas? I never took you as a Vegas girl."

"You know... even with me being from out west, I've never been there."

Tate smiled, kissing her again. "That makes two of us."

Can you see me?

"Do you want to use my headphones?" Tate asked as he tucked his backpack into the space beneath the seat in front of him.

It would be three hours before they landed in Las Vegas to get married. Candy and Jake blinked out to conserve energy during the flight, but they were in tow and excited about the trip, even if they were spirits.

"No, it's okay. I'd rather watch a movie." Leaning over, Hazel placed a kiss on Tate's lips before cuddling up next to him with the pillow and blanket they had brought from home.

Tate's family understood why they wanted to tie the knot in Vegas, and only requested they have a small family get together once they returned home. It was a small price to pay so they could save money on a wedding, and not have to go through all the planning and all the entertaining that went along with throwing a large party. They had an appointment at a small wedding chapel, as well as reservations at the Bellagio, and they were excited to spend a few days in a new city enjoying each other, minus the murder cases that usually plagued their lives.

Finding a movie on the small televisions in front of them, they purchased the airplane headphones and plugged in to watch the movie together.

***

Turbulence rocked the plane violently, pulling her out of her slumber as the overhead bins began swinging open, losing their contents onto the floor. The pilot asked them to remain calm and fasten their seatbelts, claiming the storm would pass quickly, but she wasn't convinced. Her heart hammered in her ears as she reached for his hand, looking for comfort and reassurance, but he wasn't there. Her heart became heavier as the taste of dread rose into her mouth.

Where is he? The bathroom?

Frantically, she tried to look over the seats behind her, but she couldn't see the bathroom doors over the other panicking people who sat between her and the back of the plane. She wouldn't be able to see with her seatbelt, but she was ordered to keep it on. Fighting with what to do, she tried to steady her breaths. A baby a few aisles away was screaming and crying, making her anxiety worse.

She had to take off her seatbelt; she had to find him. Swallowing the bitter taste in her mouth, she slipped off her seatbelt and rose from her seat. The plane was empty. The sound of her heartbeat had become a steady buzzing in her ears.

Where is everyone? How is the plane empty?

She spun around to look at the seats in the plane's front, but they were empty as well. A chill ran down the center of her body, numbing her. Leaving her seat, she stumbled into the aisle, unsure where she could go but knowing she needed to leave. The seats were empty.

What was that?

The sound of humming came from the last aisle, but she couldn't see who was making the sound. Gingerly, she held her breath as she walked towards the voice.

Chestnut hair in pigtails appeared over the back of the second to last seat. She hesitated, too afraid *to approach the girl. The humming stopped and was replaced by a low "Can you see me?"*

Her breath hitched. Nausea rose into her throat. Approaching the back row of seats, her blood ran cold.

"Bella?"

To be continued...

Afterword

If you liked this book, please leave a review on Amazon and Goodreads! Thank you!

***

<u>Justice for the Slain</u> (*Hazel Watson Mystery Book Two*), is available NOW!
After surviving an abduction and near death herself, Hazel, along with her police officer boyfriend, Tate, and Candy, are looking forward to their brand of normalcy.

But the spirit of a murdered man shows up in Hazel's apartment. He's not just any man, however. He's the man Candy was murdered over. This, once again, throws their world into chaos, causing her to rethink what had never been questioned.

Did the police have the right man in prison?
Hazel tests powers she never knew she had and

finds herself caught up in a tangled case of obsession and murder. The more she navigates the killer's past, the more entangled her life becomes, until it endangers those she loves. Forced to put those closest to her in the line of fire, Hazel marches into the dangerous world of a psychotic killer, to put their havoc to an end before it's too late.

***

The Prequel to *Hazel Watson Mystery Book One*, titled **Kindred Spirits**, is available on paperback and Kindle Unlimited! It not only includes the original story from Hazel's point of view, but also includes a short story from Candy's point of view as well as a third short story!

There may be more to an empty room than meets the eye. You may just find that you're not alone.

NOW WITH THREE NOVELETTES!

Candy's Story

Candy Townsend enjoyed her life as a young bartender in the city of New Orleans. Sure, she had a complicated relationship with her ex-boyfriend, Brad, but she was in love with a new man and was hopeful for the future. Sadly, her life, and her future, changed forever after one fateful night. Candy struggled in her new state of being, until nearly a year later, when a young woman with a special ability entered her apartment. A young woman named Hazel Watson.

***

Hazel's Story

Hazel Watson had newly graduated from law school and it was time for her to move into her own apartment and join the adult world. Something she was admittedly dreading. Unfortunately, the only place she could afford in the popular city of New Orleans had a reputation for being haunted. Undeterred, and desperate to find a place of her own, she moved in regardless. Using her hereditary ability to communicate with the dead, she befriends her new apartment's resident ghost and teams up with the feisty spirit to help other lost souls she encounters.

***

Haunted Holiday: The Soldier in the Stone Room

Settled into a new apartment with her spirit, best-friend, Candy, Hazel Watson prepares for her first Christmas as a fully functional adult. Her career as an attorney at the Public Defender's office was demanding, so a little rest and relaxation was on her agenda. What Hazel does not need is a new ghost in her life, or a new obligation. So, when the spirit of a Confederate soldier shows up in her dreams, and in her bedroom, Hazel must figure out who he is and how he died so he can move on.

***

Hazel Watson Mystery Book One, <u>The Sapphire Necklace</u>, is available now on paperback and Kindle Unlimited!

Still fresh to the community of public defenders, Miss Hazel Watson finds herself entangled in a case of embezzlement-with a liberal dash of the supernatural. Who was this spirit haunting her client? Why is this spirit's glimmering sapphire necklace so entrancing? And, most importantly, why could Hazel not communicate with her?

Since she was a young girl, Hazel had been helping spirits conclude their earthly business so they could pass over. Her ability to communicate with spirits was passed down from her mother, who was able to help guide her and hone her necromancy skills. Hazel was never a social butterfly, but she never had a problem communicating with the dead. Until now.

There are enough challenges being a young,

female, public attorney. Still, this new case presents challenges Hazel could never have anticipated.

As Mr. Miller's trial date inches closer, with more questions than answers, Hazel, with the help of her spectral best-friend, Candy, are rushing against the clock to identify the dead woman, find her killer, and avoid becoming the killer's next victim herself.

Acknowledgements

Thank you to my family for their support. I love you!

* * *

Thank you to my amazing editor, Bambi Sommers. You are a delight to work with!

* * *

Thank you to Sandi for helping me with proofreading!

* * *

Thank you to author Jenna Moreci, for your amazing YouTube channel and Skillshare classes. I know that I'm not the only writer who had a dream of becoming a published author, but was intimidated, until we came across you! Your YouTube channel has not only made me laugh my ass off, but has also taught me so much, and gave me the courage that I needed to 'write the damn book,' so thank you! Oh, and

your Savior series ROCKS! I've already read it
twice.

* * *

Thank you to author, E.E. Holmes, for
inspiring me with your Gateway series, and for
being a great friend! The Gateway series was the
first paranormal fiction series that I read since I
was a teen, and it blew my mind. I knew it was
where I needed to be. It was what I needed to
read, and it was what I needed to write. Thank
you so much for creating that world. It meant
more than you know. I can't wait for the new
book!!! I just miss the gang so much!

* * *

Thank you to all of my readers! I hope that
you all enjoyed this fourth book of Hazel,
Candy and Tate's story. I'm currently working
on an Epic Fantasy novel titled **The Crown of
the Phoenix**, but I am not done with Hazel's
story! More will be coming soon!

Meet the Author

C. A. Varian was raised in Lockport, Louisiana, into an often-low-income household. She spent a lot of her childhood fishing, crabbing, and playing school. She loved pretending to be the teacher and assigning work to her cousins. Her love of reading started very young, where she used to complete several books per week in elementary school so she could earn a free personal pizza from Pizza Hut. Even once free pizzas were no longer an option, she still steadily read novels, usually above the reading level for her age group, and loved visiting the library to stock up on books. She started writing poetry and short stories while still in junior high through high school, although she stopped writing, at least for fun, once she had children and went to college. Thankfully, her writing hiatus ended, and she resumed her love for writing.

She earned a Bachelor of Arts degree in History, as well as a Master's degree in History. She also worked towards getting her teaching certification. She did almost all of her college education while also being the mother of two children. After graduating from college, she began teaching public school, a career that she continues to this day, currently teaching special education at a local middle school.

She's married to a retired military officer, so she spent many years moving around for his career, but they now live in central Alabama, with her youngest daughter, Arianna. Her oldest daughter, Brianna, no longer lives at home and is engaged to be married. She has two Shih Tzus that she considers her children. Boy, Charlie, and girl, Luna, are their mommy's shadows. She also has three cats: Ramses, Simba, and Cookie, as well as five chickens and two ducks.